BRIDGERS 2: THE COST OF SURVIVAL

STAN C. SMITH

ISBN-13: 978-1720762492

ISBN-10: 172076249X

*To those who think twice before sacrificing
what they know to be moral and just.*

THE COST OF SURVIVAL

You don't get to decide who's right and who's wrong. No time for that. And it wouldn't matter anyway, because that's all made-up shit.

INFINITY FOWLER

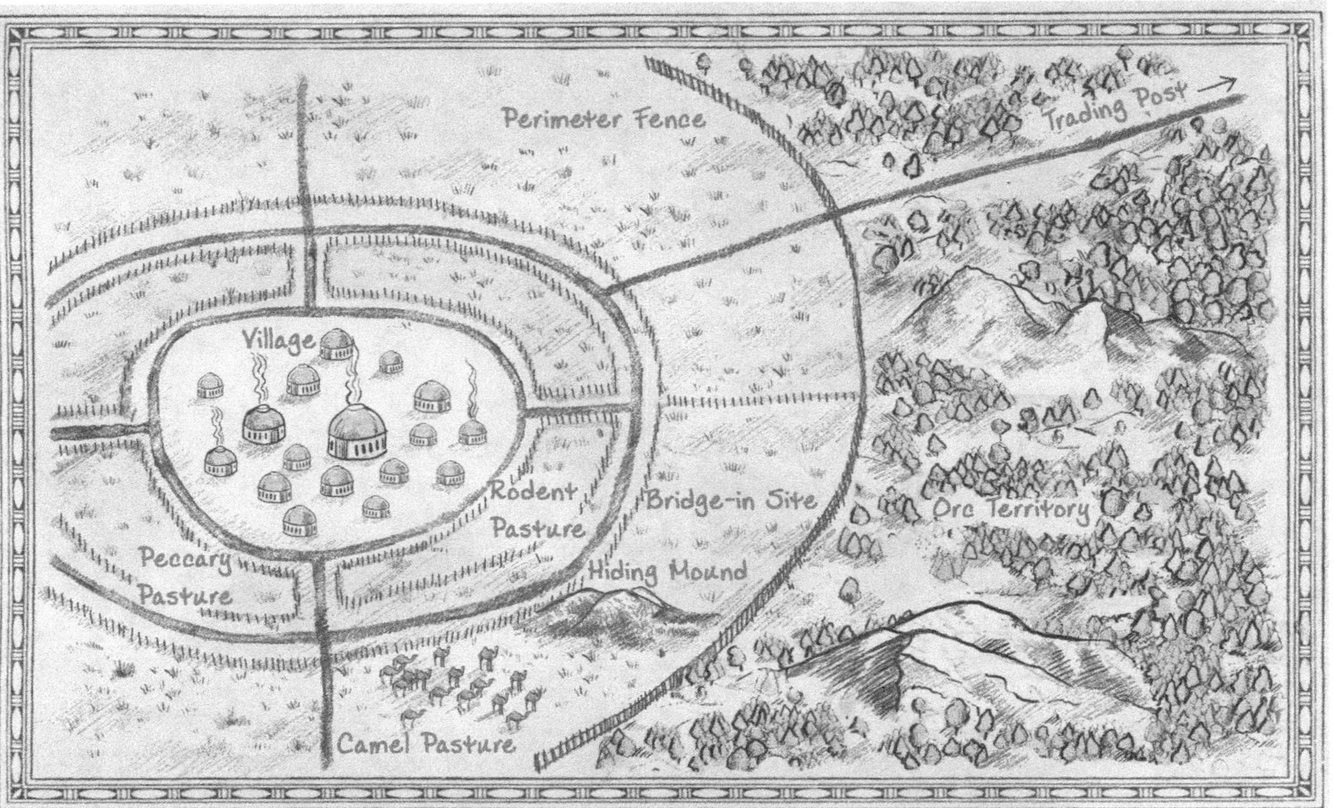

Perimeter Fence
Trading Post →
Village
Rodent Pasture
Bridge-in Site
Orc Territory
Peccary Pasture
Hiding Mound
Camel Pasture

1

———

STORM

August 24 - 9:54 AM

AUGUST COULD BE hot in Missouri, but knowing there would never be another August in this place made it seem more tolerable. Infinity Fowler stopped at the base of a towering sycamore tree and stared up into the branches. When she spotted what she was looking for, she leapt up and hooked her fingers over the lowest limb and swung her legs up and over. Seconds later, she stood upright with her bare feet gripping the smooth-barked surface. She climbed another ten feet, carefully avoiding scratches to her bare skin, as she was wearing only shorts and a sports top.

Hitched to the main trunk with a piece of wire was a triangular trapeze handle attached to a steel cable, which in turn was fastened to a thick branch fifty feet higher. Infinity untwisted the wire to free the handle. She then focused her attention on a second trapeze handle forty feet away, dangling free from a another sycamore. It was just far enough for her momentum to swing her out to where she could grab it.

Infinity had built this workout station between bridging excursions the previous winter, when few tourists were willing to bridge to alternate versions of Earth during the cold months. It was one of eight stations she had hidden in the 400 acres of dense forest surrounding the main building of SafeTrek Bridging. This forest was where Infinity and the other bridgers trained tourists, although training was little more than giving them enough experience to be less likely to kill themselves on their thirty-six-hour excursion.

Infinity closed her eyes and visualized swinging out and catching the other handle. Falling was not an option—she was out here alone, and no one knew where she was.

An unexpected gust of wind caused her to totter, and she opened her eyes and grabbed a limb to steady herself. She looked up. Dark clouds were moving in. Abrupt weather changes like this were becoming frequent, and in just the past three weeks, the news that Earth was imploding had been promoted from disturbing prediction to indisputable fact. Predictions that the process would take years had been changed to months. All hell was breaking loose, in society as well as in nature.

But in this forest, Infinity was still able to find some calm.

She sucked in a lungful of muggy air and launched herself from the limb. She swung to the other cable and grabbed its handle. She jostled to a stop, suspended by both cables, one handle in each hand. Gazing at the endless green foliage, she systematically cleared her mind of all thoughts of violence and mayhem. This had always been difficult, because Infinity was a fundamentally violent person.

After hanging this way for over a minute, she grunted and drew the two handles closer together. She threw her knees up and inverted her body, feet toward the sky. With sweat already beading from the strain, she put her left foot through the triangle handle in her left hand and then her right foot through the handle in her right. She hooked her legs over the handles by bending her knees and let go with her hands. Hanging upside down, she crossed her arms at her chest and closed her eyes. This inverted meditation state was the only long-term habit she had kept from a brief exploration of Shaolin Kung Fu.

Heart to blood, muscle to bone, tourist flesh above my own.

With self-sacrifice near, my fuel is fear.

By bridger means and might, tourists will not fight.

I aspire to inspire before I expire.

Bide within the law I must, in untainted tourist trust.

The five principles of the bridgers' creed always came to the surface of her thoughts in the first seconds of inverted meditation. Infinity had survived longer than any other bridger—nearly four years—and during that time, the principles had become woven into her identity. She had been plucked from a brutal existence in low-level professional fighting and given a chance to do something she could be proud of—protecting the lives of tourists.

But now the rules were changing.

Another blast of wind shoved her into a wobbly swing. She kept her eyes shut, trying to maintain her concentration. A faint roar gradually grew louder—a storm front was coming. The roar's intensity increased, but it wasn't just wind. Impacts on the foliage and the ground sounded like a kettle of popping corn. Still, Infinity held her eyes shut, determined to use the falling hail to her advantage. With any luck, the hailstones would be big enough to hurt. Pain was, after all, the path to self-discipline.

Pebbles of ice began pelting her legs and back, a prickly, mostly pleasant assault on her skin. Infinity smiled.

A deeper, more menacing roar materialized and drew nearer, forcing her to finally open her eyes. What the hell was it? Seconds later the onslaught was upon her. A much larger hailstone struck her knee. She cursed and glanced up at it. Blood was trickling from a gash in her skin.

Hailstones the size of apples pummeled the trees above and the ground below, and the leaves and twigs fell around her like confetti. A chunk of ice struck her shin, almost hard enough to crack the bone. She had to find shelter. Bending at the waist, she grabbed the two handles and struggled to pull her feet out.

A hailstone smashed into her forehead above her right eye, and she fell.

Infinity was barely aware of her reflexes taking over, twisting her body to avoid landing on her head. She fell fifteen feet and hit the ground on her side. A hailstone struck her hip and another hit her knee. Instinctively, she covered her head with her arms. Still dazed, she crawled to the base of the sycamore and pressed against the trunk for shelter.

The barrage of hail was deafening, but then an even more intense wave of sound approached, accompanied by the cracking of tree limbs. Wind blasted past Infinity, forcing the falling hailstones into a diagonal path. A nearby tree crashed to the ground, and she hugged the sycamore even tighter.

The massive trunk changed shape, its thickness bulging outward against her body. And then it exploded. The splintering wood assaulted Infinity's senses like a bomb going off beside her. She rolled away from the tree and a fragment the size of her arm struck her shoulder as it flew from the fracturing trunk. The entire tree collapsed, taking down two others with it.

Hail pelted the ground around her, and more trees were falling. Infinity realized the only shelter was under the fallen sycamore, its thick trunk now held several feet above the ground by what remained of its largest branches. She crawled, taking a painful hit to her back before tucking herself beneath the trunk.

The storm raged on for what seemed like twenty minutes. Pulverized leaves and hailstones accumulated on the ground, creating seas of white and green between the shattered trunks of fallen trees.

And then the storm stopped, just as abruptly as it had started.

Infinity didn't move until she saw shafts of sunlight illuminating the devastated forest. She rolled from beneath the tree and got up. Pink gashes dotted her skin, but otherwise she was okay. What about the SafeTrek building? And what about the 2,000 refugees and workers living in tents and campers beside the half-mile road leading to SafeTrek's front door? Infinity took off toward the building. But the forest before her was now a wasteland. She had to pick her way over and around fallen trees.

Finally, she emerged from the ravaged forest onto the training field behind the facility. Normally mowed and manicured, it was now strewn with leaves, limbs, and manmade debris. The wooden picnic table was missing. SafeTrek's block-like building appeared to be unharmed. Infinity wondered about the power generators on the roof. If they were destroyed, this would be a setback in SafeTrek's efforts to save the human species from extinction. And it would almost certainly result in Infinity and the other bridgers dying along with everyone else.

She ran to the back door. The rock she had used earlier to keep the door from latching was gone, so the door was now locked. She headed around the east side of the building.

Hints of the destruction came into view as soon as she rounded the corner. And she could already hear cries of anguish and pain. When she came to the building's front corner, she stopped. The scene before her was complete chaos. Nearly every tent, camper, bunkhouse trailer, food booth, and portable toilet was overturned or flattened. Debris was everywhere. And so were bodies. Refugees and workers who were unharmed were helping the injured, although some were standing in place or wandering around in shock.

"Infinity! I need your help." It was Poppy Safran, one of the med techs.

Infinity ran to her side. Poppy was kneeling over a man with a bloodied face and body.

"I think his trachea is crushed," Poppy said. "If you squeeze it right here in just the right way, he can get enough air. But I need to help others. There are so many, Infinity. I just... I have to help them." Her eyes were wide, and tears streaked her face.

Infinity knelt beside her and took the man's throat. "I've got it, Poppy. Go."

Without another word, the med tech got up and ran toward the sound of several people screaming.

Infinity turned to the injured man. He was grasping desperately at her hand on his throat, unable to breathe. She squeezed, expanding the trachea, and air rushed into his lungs. The guy's face was a mess, and it looked like he may have lost one of his eyes. Perhaps he'd been knocked out by one of the hailstones and then, lying unconscious, had taken the full force of twenty minutes of fist-sized chunks of ice.

"Just relax and breathe," she said. "Panic will make it worse."

There was no way the guy could speak, but apparently he could hear, because he loosened his grip on her wrist and slowed his breathing.

With her free hand, she guided his fingers to hers. "Listen to me," she said firmly. "I want you to do this yourself. That way you can adjust the pressure as needed. Do you feel where my fingers are?"

He nodded slightly.

"Okay, I'm going to let go." She pulled her hand away.

He choked for a moment and then got the pressure to where he could breathe.

"You're going to be okay," she said. "Now, stay calm and don't move. More help will be here soon."

She left him on the ground and walked to the road. A quarter mile away, the road curved to the left and out of sight behind the ravaged trees. But everything she could see in that quarter mile was at least partially destroyed. How many had been injured or killed?

These people had been selected to be survivors of the human species, to be bridged to alternate worlds in groups of 718. The tragedy of this goddamn storm would be far greater than today's deaths.

Ahead on the side of the road, a group of twenty or so people were rolling an overturned RV back onto its wheels. Once it was upright, several men yanked the door open and rushed inside to help the occupants. The others began dispersing to provide assistance elsewhere. Infinity recognized one of them just as he spotted her.

Desmond ran to her. "Infinity!" He looked like he was about to hug her, but then he stopped short. "I couldn't find you in the building. I was afraid you were out training and got caught in the storm." He then seemed to notice the gashes and mud covering her body. "I guess you did get caught in the storm."

Desmond was Infinity's new bridging partner. And she might have wanted him to be more to her than that if the world weren't going to hell.

"I'm fine," she said. "The National Guardsmen were supposed to be here three days ago! Where the hell are they? We're eighteen miles from the nearest hospital and we don't have the facilities or personnel to—"

"Doyle told us they're on their way now," he said.

Armando Doyle was Infinity's boss and SafeTrek's CEO. Or at least he had been until the government had taken control of the facility to bridge as many refugees to alternate worlds as possible.

"I'm glad you're okay," Desmond said.

Infinity ignored this and stared out at the chaos. Shouts, crying, and the clattering of debris being moved came from every direction at once. "Where do we even begin?"

"Bridgers! Bridgers!"

They turned to see a woman in filthy clothes approaching. Blood was smeared on her face, but Infinity recognized her—

Lorissa Allport. She was one of two scientists Infinity and Desmond had been training for the next bridging excursion to verify a habitable version of Earth.

"Thank God you two are okay," Lorrisa said as she stopped before them. "We're still on track for our excursion, right? Will this storm delay things?"

Infinity stared at her for a moment and then exchanged a glance with Desmond.

"Are you serious?" Desmond asked.

Lorissa looked at the ground briefly. "I don't mean to appear callous, but I'd like to know if we're still on schedule."

2

———————

BIO-PROBE

August 24 - 8:20 PM

DESMOND STARED at the painted concrete ceiling of his bunk room. Previously, he had considered the stark, utilitarian design of the SafeTrek building to be ugly and uninspired. But the structure had been built to endure almost anything, and after the freakish storm today—massive hail and 90 mph straight-line winds— Desmond had a new appreciation for the design.

He needed sleep. But there wasn't a single aspect of his life that wasn't careening balls-to-the-wall out of control. When he had bridged to another version of Earth a few weeks ago, he'd been tortured by bird-like creatures and had nearly died half a dozen times. Thanks to SafeTrek's med techs, he was now quickly recovering. But how could he recover from what he now knew to be true? And from what he'd seen today?

Hours after the storm had devastated the makeshift city of refugees, nearly 2,000 members of the Army National Guard from Fort Leonard Wood and several other bases in Missouri had finally arrived. By that time, Desmond's mind and soul had become numbed by his attempts at helping triage uncountable injuries. Some of the injuries defied explanation, including a seemingly-intact human brain he'd found lying in the grass beneath a mangled piece of camper siding. How was that even possible?

The storm had come with no warning. And as devastating as it had been, it was only one of many extreme weather events happening everywhere. Other places had seen much worse. Not only that, but other places were occupied by people with little hope. At least the refugees gathered here had been selected to bridge to alternate worlds. They had some chance of surviving the now-certain implosion of the planet. Desmond couldn't even imagine the state of despair that must exist beyond the guarded boundaries of SafeTrek's property.

He thought of his mom. She was still trying to live a normal life. Every day, she went to her office on the University of Kentucky campus, although students had stopped showing up over a week ago. Desmond had been trying to get her a spot in one of the refugee groups, but it was like shouting into a hurricane. Everyone on the planet wanted a spot. But he wasn't going to give up.

Almost by accident, Desmond had become a bridger. He was now Infinity's partner. SafeTrek had three pairs of bridgers. They used to protect the lives of tourists, but now their purpose was to find suitable worlds for colonies of 718 refugees per world.

He sighed, got up from his bunk, and stared into the mirror. He ran his fingers through several weeks of hair growth on his scalp. "You're an imposter," he said aloud.

He glanced at the clock. There was a mandatory meeting at 9:00 PM, but he had time to stop by and see Lenny and Xavier. He shoved his feet into his sandals and left his bunk room.

He found both of his friends in Lenny's room.

"Come on in, Des," Lenny said.

Lenny was sitting in the chair by the small desk, so Desmond sat on the bunk next to Xavier.

Xavier held out a white plastic flask. "It's JD Black."

Desmond stared at it. "You're kidding, right?"

"I brought a couple with me," Lenny said. "I figured we'd need a little after our excursion." He shook his head. "I should've brought a lot more."

Desmond looked his two college roommates over. They hadn't even showered yet. Both were smeared with the blood of injured or dead refugees. They had both been hurt on a recent disastrous bridging expedition with Desmond and each still had a cast on one leg, but they had insisted on helping until the guardsmen had taken over.

"Give me that." Desmond took the flask and allowed himself one swallow. He handed it back. "I've got a meeting in a few minutes, and then the bio-probe is returning at 1:00 AM."

They stared at him, frowning.

"Freaking unbelievable," Lenny said.

Desmond shook his head. "It's not at all unbelievable. The generators and the bridging device are undamaged. I talked to Lorissa Allport today. She was more horrified that we might cancel the excursion than she was about the storm killing over a hundred of her refugee group."

Xavier blew out a puff of air. "God almighty. This is worse than any nightmare."

Lenny took the flask from Xavier and raised it up. "I envy you, Des. You're guaranteed a position in a colony." He took a drink.

"So are both of you," Desmond said. "When your legs heal."

Lenny swallowed and grimaced at the burn. "There may not be that much time left, brother."

9:00 PM

WHEN DESMOND ARRIVED at the meeting room, Infinity was waiting in the hall beside the open door. Like him, she had cleaned up. But in spite of her tough exterior and a lifetime of brutal fighting, there was a hollowness to her stare Desmond hadn't seen before.

He stopped beside her and spoke softly. "Any tips for this meeting?"

"They may not care about our opinions. We're only bridgers. But if they ask, tell them what you think. And if they don't ask, tell them anyway."

He waited for more. "That's it?"

She shrugged. "This is all new territory."

They entered the room and sat at the table.

It was a small group. Next to Armando Doyle was Celia Pickett, Doyle's competent assistant. Next to her were Lorissa and Zachariah, the two scientists selected to determine the viability of the alternate world for the 718 refugees they represented. Finally, there was a fifty-something guy in a suit, no doubt from the federal government, since SafeTrek had been more-or-less commandeered by the Feds.

Once they were seated, Doyle gazed at Infinity. "Should I be concerned about you?"

She frowned slightly and shook her head.

There was an interesting connection between Infinity and the much-older Doyle that Desmond hadn't quite figured out. At times, the SafeTrek CEO seemed to dote upon her, almost like a father would. Desmond hoped it was nothing more than that.

Doyle addressed the room. "It's been a long day for all of us. But we have a bio-probe returning at 1:00 AM, and difficult decisions have to be made. It is my intent to hear all of your opinions and weigh them carefully as we move forward."

The guy in the suit cleared his throat. "If you don't mind, Armando, I'm going to just tell the plain and unvarnished truth about our situation."

Doyle sighed. "If you haven't met him yet, this is Reece Eagleton, Regional Administrator of FEMA. He is the current liaison between the government and SafeTrek."

"I will add," Eagleton said, "that I am working under the direct orders of President Hayley Millright. Never in our nation's history have Americans had to face anything like what we're currently dealing with."

"Everyone is facing this, not just Americans," Infinity said. "Just tell us what we have to do."

Eagleton pursed his lips for a moment. "Of course." He then went on. "With every passing day, the disaster is magnified. Frankly, we have no idea how much longer our essential infrastructure will hold out. SafeTrek is one of three bridging facilities in the U.S." He glanced at Infinity and added, "And one of seven around the globe. Building these facilities was a terrible mistake. For the record, I was against their construction from the beginning. But now, ironically, these facilities are the only hope for saving a small portion of the human race. A *very* small portion."

Infinity actually slammed her hand on the table. But then she shook her head, apparently deciding not to say what she was thinking.

Eagleton glared at her. "You want me to get to the point? Alright. We're running out of time. In spite of today's disaster, there will be no delays. In fact, there will be no delays for as long as this facility continues to function. The moment we have a successful bio-probe, we will send an assessment team. The moment the team returns with news of a suitable world, we'll begin sending refugees. This must happen as rapidly as possible."

Desmond shifted in his seat, unsure he wanted to speak up but deciding he had to. "Today, 132 refugees from the next group in line were killed, and more were injured."

Eagleton nodded. "We've already reconfigured by combining the survivors from both groups that were waiting outside. There are more than enough for the next colony. And in a few days, we'll have two more groups on-site. And more after that. You keep the facility running, we'll keep bringing all the refugees you can handle."

"Can I say something?" It was Zachariah Thorp. "As a parasitologist, I've been assigned to help assess the suitability of a destination world." He nodded toward Desmond and Infinity. "Lorissa and I will accompany these bridgers on the assessment excursion. It is my opinion that when we return from the excursion, I will need a significant amount of time to determine whether or not we have encountered harmful parasites."

"I understand your concern," Eagleton said, although with no trace of empathy. "After returning, you will be given sixty minutes to make a decision."

Zachariah's mouth fell open. "That's outrageous! I can't possibly—"

"I have to agree with Mr. Eagleton," Lorissa said. "If there's anything to be learned from the events of today, it is that time is crucial."

Zachariah's face reddened. "You don't need time after we've returned because you're an agricultural scientist. Your evaluation will be completed on-site."

Eagleton held up his hands as if it would calm everyone. "Your concerns are noted. But I also want to point out that it is late August. Winter will be arriving in a few short months, not only here but on every world we send refugees to. The colonies will be starting with nothing. They will need time to prepare for winter."

Eagleton paused as if making sure they understood the significance of this. "When the bio-probe returns later tonight, you'll have sixty minutes to determine if the world is worth an exploratory excursion. After you return from the excursion, you'll have sixty minutes to decide if the world is suitable for your refugees. And you can be assured of this: we are lowering the bar for what qualifies as a viable world."

Infinity pushed her chair back and stood up. "Maybe you all need more of the truth. Everyone who stays here dies—you seem to understand that. But I've bridged to a shitload of alternate worlds. I've been lucky to survive every time. But only because I returned here, where we have good med equipment and great med techs. Now you want to bridge 718 people naked and empty-handed to an alternate world, and they have to stay there forever?" She let this question hang there as if daring them to formulate an answer. She then turned and left the room.

The meeting was over.

———

AUGUST 25 - 12:35 AM

THE SAME GROUP of people from the 9:00 PM meeting gathered in the viewing room adjacent to the bridging chamber. But no one seemed interested in conversing. Desmond was beyond tired, so perhaps the others were too.

Doyle seemed unusually somber, so his assistant Celia took over the explanations. "The bio-probe is a relatively simple concept," she explained, although Desmond was pretty sure Lorissa and Zachariah already knew what a bio-probe was. "Basically, the device randomly selects one world from an infinite array of alternate worlds. The only thing we select is the divergence point, or how far back in time the destination universe diverged from our own. Once we have a world and a divergence point, we bridge six pairs of test animals: Dorset sheep, domestic cats, rabbits, guinea pigs, rats, and mice. Thirty-six hours later, the twelve test animals automatically bridge back to this chamber, regardless of their location on the other world, and regardless of their physical state. If they return alive, that indicates the world is habitable by mammals."

Desmond noticed Doyle was gazing with raised brows at the FEMA guy, Eagleton. Eagleton shrugged and nodded.

"Excuse me, Celia," Doyle said. He then faced the two scientists. "Normally we don't reveal this information until after you have signed nondisclosure agreements. But none of that really matters now."

He went on to explain what the general public did not know, that the technology behind the bridging devices was not human technology. It had come from the extraterrestrial radio signal discovered five years ago, sent from the mysterious alien race now known as the Outlanders. In other words, humans really had no idea how the devices worked.

Not surprisingly, this was met with shock then disbelief and then anger. But the overall tone of the discussion was quite different from how it had taken place over three weeks ago when Desmond, Lenny, and Xavier had learned this disturbing news. That had been a different time, when excursions were optional and humans thought they had all the time in the world.

When Zachariah and Lorissa seemed finally to come to grips with this revelation, it was followed by news regarding a second radio signal, which had been discovered only three weeks ago. The second signal had been transmitted by yet another extraterrestrial civilization, and it contained a warning. Unfortunately, Earth's radio telescopes had discovered the first signal before discovering the second. The second signal would have warned humans that constructing and activating bridging devices created an unusual and very dense type of submicroscopic particle, which would begin a chain reaction that couldn't be stopped. But now it was too late. These particles had drifted to the planet's core, causing every other particle they touched to disappear, perhaps bridging them to other universes. This was gradually diminishing the planet's core. The early symptoms were earthquakes, extreme weather events, and disruption of the magnetosphere. The final symptoms were uncertain, but it didn't take much imagination to realize the planet's core would gradually disappear. Gravity would collapse the crust to fill the void. This was already happening but would soon escalate to unimaginable intensity.

It could only be assumed that the Outlanders' radio signal had been designed intentionally to destroy other civilizations. It offered an irresistible technology as bait, and humans had taken it hook, line, and sinker. The only escape was the very technology that was destroying the earth.

The already grim mood in the room devolved into wretched despondency.

"It's almost time," Celia said. She pointed to the thick plexiglass that separated them from the bridging chamber. "The test animals will appear in the center of the chamber, just above the floor."

They all stepped toward the window and waited silently.

The plexiglass bulged outward slightly, and then the animals appeared and fell to the floor. The first few seconds were chaotic as the hairless, frightened creatures scrambled over each other and scattered, some of them running headlong into the walls.

Desmond kept his eyes on the floor in the center of the chamber. Only one test animal remained there, motionless. Perhaps it had been a rabbit, although it was hard to tell. Now it was a pile of white bones and dark, formless flesh.

The airlock hatch opened, and techs in white biosuits poured into the chamber to catch and examine the panicked animals.

Armando Doyle seemed to perk up. "Excellent! A highly-successful bio-probe. This makes the decision quite easy. We will begin preparing for you to bridge at 7:00 AM."

"No," Eagleton said forcefully. "This is not a tourist excursion. We don't have time to wait six hours. The bridge will take place in sixty minutes."

Doyle shook his head. "That's not a prudent—"

Infinity turned away from the window and glared menacingly at Eagleton. "Maybe you don't understand how this works. We're bridging to another version of our own planet. Same time, same place. But we have no idea what we'll encounter there. If you want us to arrive there in the dark at two in the morning, then you're coming with us. You willing to do that?"

Eagleton's eyes narrowed and his face darkened. "Young lady, perhaps you don't realize the urgency—"

"That's the goddamn deal!" She stepped toward him, and Eagleton's eyes widened. "If you want to come, we bridge in an hour. If not, how about you let those who know what they're doing make this decision."

Lorissa said, "Um, Infinity, whatever we can do to speed this up—"

"Stop talking, tourist!" Infinity continued glaring at Eagleton, her muscles tensed like she was ready to pounce. If Eagleton had seen the things Desmond had seen Infinity do, he'd proceed with caution.

Doyle wisely spoke up. "I'm supporting Infinity on this, Reece. She's a damn good bridger, and she knows better than to bridge into darkness."

Desmond's eye caught movement beyond the plexiglass. One of the white-suited techs was waving his arm to get their attention.

Doyle stepped over and pressed a button on the wall, activating the comm system.

"Cursory examination reveals good physical health in all but one test-animal, sir," the tech said. "One rabbit appears to have been butchered."

Doyle glanced at Infinity and back to the tech. "Butchered?"

"I could be wrong, but the carcass shows signs of cutting with a sharpened tool. The meat was removed from the bones. But all the others appear unharmed. No signs of extreme temperatures, submersion in water, or excessive UV radiation."

Again Doyle turned to Infinity. "What do you think?"

"Sir, there's one other thing," the tech said. "The larger animals —the sheep, cats, and remaining rabbit—all show signs of restraint. Bruising and lacerations around the neck. Perhaps a rope or cord of some kind."

Infinity sighed loudly and rubbed the short hair on the back of her scalp. She gazed at Desmond.

Having gone on only one excursion, Desmond was hardly a real bridger. His opinion probably wouldn't matter. But he suspected they'd have little choice anyway—these were desperate times. So he nodded to Infinity.

She sighed again and turned to Doyle. "Okay." Then she shot a glance at Eagleton. "We'll bridge at 7:00 AM."

3

———————

NEVERLAND

August 25 - 6:40 AM

Infinity downed the last of the water in her bottle as she and Desmond passed through the air lock to the lab adjacent to the bridging chamber. She glanced at Desmond's bottle. "Finish that now, otherwise you'll lose most of it when we bridge."

For reasons humans didn't understand, substances that weren't part of the body disappeared during the bridging process. This included food and water that had been ingested but hadn't had time to enter the cells. That's why there was no point in eating breakfast before bridging. Infinity hadn't eaten since the previous morning—there hadn't been time. So she was already hungry, which was a lousy way to start a thirty-six-hour excursion.

Wraith and Trencher were in the lab, pulling on their clothes. The two bridgers had just completed three days of mandatory chemo-cleansing and patho-cleansing. They were finishing the same process Infinity and Desmond were about to begin: bridging to a world that had returned a positive bio-probe, spending thirty-six hours confirming the world's viability, and then immediately bridging back to the same world for another thirty-six hours, during which 718 refugees were bridged to the world twenty at a time. Doing two excursions back-to-back was insane. But this was the new job bridgers had been given. And it would continue that way until the end.

"Bridgers," Infinity said as she approached them. She leaned forward. Wraith leaned down and pressed his forehead to hers, and then Trencher did the same. This ritual had been started a few years ago by a bridger named Hornet. It was an unspoken acknowledgement of the skill and resolve of any bridger returning alive. The ritual lived on, even though Hornet had eventually returned from an excursion half eaten by a predator.

Infinity looked them over. "No serious injuries. Was it a neverland?"

A neverland was what bridgers called any alternate world that was free of danger and hardships—a paradise, in other words. Unfortunately, none of them had ever actually found one.

Wraith grunted and shook his head. "Divergence point of two hundred years, so definitely human-occupied. We found a gravel road, but there were no recent tracks on it, and we never saw a vehicle or anything else come by."

Trencher pulled a faded SafeTrek t-shirt on over his head. "We never saw another soul. As far as we knew, the zombie apocalypse could have happened during the last two hundred years and wiped them all out. Babysitting each refugee group as they arrived didn't give us a chance to scout out very far."

Wraith said, "I swear to God, Infinity, every one of them had the dry heaves after bridging. Twenty at a time. Another fresh group every hour." He shook his head. "Damn."

"We had no choice but to leave them all there," Trencher added. "They've got some good people in their group, but I don't know. I just don't know."

"And we never will," Infinity said. "You guys did what you could." She then turned to Desmond, who was now standing beside her. "I think you've met my new partner, Decay."

"You can just call me Desmond," he said.

Wraith and Trencher nodded but didn't say anything, which pissed Infinity off a little. She could see it in their eyes—they wondered why Desmond had suddenly been made a bridger. Like Infinity, they had both had years of hand-to-hand combat training and experience. Desmond hadn't, and he didn't look much like a bridger. But he had surprised Infinity with his ingenuity and guts. And he had saved her life. So she really didn't care what the other bridgers thought.

Wraith turned back to Infinity. "Good luck, sister. I hope you get a neverland."

"Damn right," Trencher added. "You're due for one."

Infinity nodded and turned away. She was definitely due for a neverland. She had lost her partner in each of her last two excursions, one to a poison dart and one to a predator.

Armando was escorting the two tourist-scientists through the airlock, and when they cleared the second hatch, they joined Infinity and Desmond at the hatch to the bridging chamber.

As he often did before sending bridgers and tourists to their possible deaths, Armando attempted to be cheerful. He clapped his hands together and glanced at his watch. "All right, then! I trust you've all had your radioisotope doses?"

He was talking about technetium-99m, the radioisotope marker. Each person bridging had to have both an injection and an oral dose of the stuff. No one knew exactly how, but its radioactive decay triggered the bridging device to pull you back to your own world after exactly thirty-six hours and 3.6 seconds.

They all nodded. Zachariah and Lorissa both looked pale. At least they were smart enough to be scared. Infinity had been assigned tourists in the past who were too stupid to know what they were really getting themselves into. She was proud of the fact that she had kept every one of the idiots alive until bridge-back.

Zachariah said, "Perhaps a bit of levity is in order. What did the male bacteria say to the female bacteria?" He forced a stupid-looking grin. "Let's convert our potential energy to kinetic energy."

In the silence that followed, Infinity wondered how this pudgy academic would handle the excursion, especially if things went south. He had pleasantly surprised her a few times during training, but that was training.

He chuckled awkwardly. "Hello? Is antibody out there?"

Again, silence.

"Sorry," he said. "I have no resistance to a dose of microbiological humor."

Finally, Armando slapped the tourist on the shoulder. "You're going to be an asset to the team, Dr. Thorp! God knows, Infinity could use some of your humor. She's wound a bit tight."

Infinity glared at him and made an exaggerated nod down toward his watch.

"Of course," Armando said. "It's nearly time." He looked around like he was about to reveal a secret. "Eagleton was hesitant to pass through the airlock. A bit of a hypocrite, if you ask me. Since he's not here, I'd like to encourage you to consider choosing a world with a more recent divergence point."

Desmond said it first. "We've already done the bio-probe for this world. It would cost us thirty-six hours to start over and probe another world. I thought Eagleton was all about saving time."

Armando nodded. "He is. But I'm not convinced he understands the potential benefits of a world with a more recent divergence point. Perhaps if you all insist, he will allow a delay for an additional bio-probe."

This had all been considered already. The reasoning was that a world with a recent divergence point would be almost identical to this world, and therefore it would have houses and buildings for shelter. And it was reasonable to think that a group of 718 refugees might be accepted and allowed to integrate into the existing society. An unpredictable and dangerous wilderness was fine for wealthy tourists seeking adventure, but not a great place to start a colony of naked humans. Actually, choosing a recent divergence point should have been a no-brainer. But in reality, except for Wraith's and Trencher's recent colony, most of the refugee groups were voting *not* to do this. There was something about human nature—an overwhelming will to be unique, to be special. When faced with the choice, refugees were choosing to risk hostile wilderness conditions in order to start their own isolated colony in a universe where humans had never existed. In Infinity's opinion, this self-righteous human trait would cost the lives of entire colonies.

"We can't do that," Lorissa said. "The colony has voted. And they voted again last night with the new replacement members. The result was decisive. A divergence point of 210,000 years. We want to be the only humans there."

Infinity wasn't sure what to think of Lorissa. She had done fine in training, but she displayed a strange mix of trying to be fiercely independent while obviously craving attention. She had personal-space issues. And she sure as hell was in a hurry to leave this world behind forever.

"Are you all in agreement?" Armando asked. He looked from one of them to the next. Zachariah and Lorissa nodded, Desmond shrugged, and Infinity just glared at him. She knew her opinion wasn't really going to matter. Armando sighed and then gestured to the open airlock hatches of the bridging chamber. They all stepped through.

Celia came in with four zippered garment bags, and they each removed their clothes and stuffed them into the bags. Infinity and Desmond had already forced the two tourists to train in the nude, so they were past the awkward-resistance phase. Celia went through the usual instructions. What it boiled down to was: follow every goddamn order from your bridgers during the first minutes after bridging. The first few minutes were critical and always confusing.

Infinity positioned the tourists a few feet apart and then faced them. "Here's the real deal. You'll drop a few inches to the ground, maybe more. And the ground may be sloped. Be ready for it so you don't fall. You'll land on your feet. But then you're going to want to throw up, although nothing much will come out. It's normal, so don't sweat it. Decay and I will assess the surroundings and decide the first course of action. Keep your mouths shut and do what we say. That's it."

They both nodded.

Celia gathered the clothes bags and left the chamber.

"Good luck to you all," Armando said. "We'll have your colony ready to bridge when you return." He then put his hand on Infinity's shoulder. "Come back alive, kiddo."

Armando had been using that nickname more often lately—not a good sign. She ignored it and nodded. "I hope there's something here for us to come back to."

He left the chamber, and one of the techs sealed the hatch.

"One minute," Celia said over the comm.

Infinity turned again to the tourists. "Put your arms out like this. It helps with the body scan and with your balance. Now bend your knees slightly—you're about to drop to the ground."

As the seconds passed, Infinity watched their faces. They were scared. She glanced at Desmond. His stance was good, and he appeared focused.

"Why do bacteria like nitrates so much?" Zachariah asked.

Silence.

"They're cheaper than day rates."

And then the bridging chamber was gone.

4

———

FENCE

August 25 - 7:00 AM

Following a prickly, gooey sensation on his skin, Desmond dropped no more than a foot onto solid ground. He'd been expecting a more violent impact, because he'd suffered a broken nose the only other time he had bridged out. He wavered on his feet for a moment before gaining his balance. The first thing he noticed was that it was pouring rain. Heavy drops pelted his scalp, which was now devoid of hair.

"Everyone okay?" Infinity asked, although her voice was almost drowned out by the pounding rain.

"I'm fine," Desmond said, and then he doubled over and retched. From the corner of his eye, he saw that Lorissa and Zachariah were doing the same thing.

"We're in an open grassy area," Infinity said, not waiting for the other two to answer. She turned. "Oh, shit! Large mammals. They're coming at us."

Desmond straightened up and looked. The creatures were less

than a hundred yards away, coming at a trot. At least fifty of them. He rubbed the rain from his eyes and squinted. "They're ungulates of some kind. Hoofed mammals."

"They don't look like predators," she said.

Perhaps they weren't predators, but they were as big as horses, and now they were running. Desmond swung around. They were in a grassy field with no shelter nearby. Then he noticed something in the distance, almost obscured by the falling rain. It took a moment for him to realize it was a fence. But then the thunderous pounding of hooves approaching behind him pulled his attention back to the immediate threat.

"You three—gather into a group!" Infinity cried.

Lorissa and Zachariah were still doubled over, but they stood up and huddled against Desmond.

"Heavens to Betsy!" Zachariah muttered in Desmond's ear as the pounding hooves grew even louder.

Infinity put herself between them and the hurtling beasts. Just as the creatures were almost upon them, she thrust out both her hands and yelled, "Stop!"

Astoundingly, just before trampling over her, the creatures did stop. Then they fanned out and surrounded the huddled group. Snuffling and grunting, they stared at the naked, hairless humans from only a few feet away. Their loose, prehensile lips flapped open and shut, producing a wet, popping sound. With every one of them doing this, the constant popping was louder than the splattering rain.

Desmond released the two scientists, but Lorissa's arm was around his neck and she was reluctant to let go. "It's okay, I think they're harmless," he said. Still he had to grab her wrist and peel her arm off. He gazed at the surrounding creatures. They had large eyes and small ears. Their feet were split into two hoof-like toes. "They're camels," he said. "Or at least related to camels."

"What do they want?" Zachariah asked. "I'm feeling a little

exposed here." He was standing with his hands cupped over his groin.

The camels were inching closer, and a pair of lips actually touched Desmond's arm. He resisted the urge to push the thing's face back, fearing he might infuriate it.

"Stand up straight," Infinity ordered. "Be defiant and don't back down."

"These are domesticated animals," Lorissa said. "Livestock. Look at their necks."

Desmond hadn't noticed before, but around each creature's neck was a twisted wire cord. And attached to the wire was a three-inch metal tag. All the animals' tags appeared to be of the same design. They had been formed into a shape that resembled a fish.

Lorissa extended a hand and cautiously patted one of them on the snout. It responded by slopping her fingers with its wet lips. Suddenly a bulging pink mass sagged out the side of it's mouth. "You're right," she said. "These are definitely camels. That thing looks like a tongue, but its actually called a *dulla*. Male camels have them."

A high-pitched call rose above the rain and the flapping camel lips, like a child shouting, "*Oak-lee-lee-lee-lee-lee! Oak-lee-lee-lee-lee-lee!*"

In unison, the camels stopped popping their lips and raised their heads to look. With the mass of bodies surrounding them, Desmond couldn't see anything. The camels all took off toward the sound, some of them actually shouldering the humans aside in their haste.

"Heavens to Betsy!" Zachariah exclaimed again.

Desmond followed Zachariah's gaze. A few hundred feet away stood three more camels. But these were festooned with ropes and tack, and saddles were fastened behind the creatures' necks at the base of their domed backs. Straddling each saddle was a human-like creature, although definitely not *Homo sapiens*. These hominids were smaller, with nearly-round faces due to an almost complete lack of forehead and only a thin mat of hair on their scalps. Their skin was dark, and they were naked from the waist up, although they wore pants that ended just below their knees. Gleaming bands of copper-colored metal adorned their wrists and upper arms, and more copper ornaments hung from their necks. One of them was a female, her breasts protruding on either side of her ornaments.

As the herd of camels cleared the area around Desmond's group, one of the male riders seemed to notice the humans standing there, and he pointed.

Just as the camels began gathering around them, the riders leaned to the side in their saddles, wheeling their camels around, and took off. The riderless camels ran after them.

"This isn't what we were hoping for," Infinity said.

Desmond watched the riders as they became increasingly obscured by the falling rain. Beyond them he saw the faint outlines of a dozen or more domed roofs. Thick smoke rose from two points within this cluster of structures.

"Do you think they're aggressive?" Zachariah asked.

Infinity wiped rainwater from her face. "Everything's aggressive when startled. And we just startled them. If you want a world that isn't occupied by humans or something human-like, then we've failed. We need to hide from them and stay hidden until bridge-back tomorrow night. Then we can bio-probe another world."

Lorissa's eyes widened. "We can't give up already! I know it's not what we wanted, but maybe these people are friendly. They may even help our colony—maybe teach us how to raise these animals, or perhaps how to farm here."

Desmond looked at Lorissa. He wasn't sure what to say, so he simply stated what he knew. "There's a town or village over there. That's where they're headed." Then he turned and pointed the other direction. "And there's a fence over that way. And now I see there's another fence that way." He pointed to his left. "We must be in an enclosure for their camels—a pasture."

"Which means we're in a cage," Infinity added. "If they return with weapons or reinforcements, the fence will slow our escape. There are trees beyond that fence. That's where we're going. Let's move."

Zachariah turned to go, but Lorissa stayed put.

Desmond saw the fire in Infinity's eyes and decided he'd better help. "Lorissa, we're not giving up. We're just being prudent. We'll get to a safer place, and then we'll be in a better position to evaluate these people. Understand?"

"I agree with the bridgers, Lorissa," Zachariah said. "This is why they're here with us."

Her face was strained, and she blinked water out of her eyes, but it was hard to tell if it was tears or rain. Finally, she nodded.

They began making their way to the fence.

The fence was farther than Desmond had thought. And as they approached it, he realized its unusual height had played a part in that illusion. When they finally stopped, it towered above them, perhaps twelve feet high. It was made of horizontal timbers no more than three inches apart, many of them sawed lengthwise so that they were roughly uniform in thickness. Their ends were fitted firmly into holes cut into massive vertical posts protruding from the ground about every six feet.

"This is overkill," Zachariah said. "It's much more than they'd need to keep the camels in."

Infinity was looking up. "That's not its only purpose."

With the horizontal slats so close together, Desmond hadn't noticed that the top of the fence on the far side extended outward several feet. And protruding down from this lip were countless sharpened spikes. The spikes were so close together that it would be extremely difficult to climb over from the other side.

"It's not just here to keep the camels in," Lorissa said. "It's to keep something out."

Desmond gazed down the fence to his right. A short distance away, something was mounted atop one of the vertical posts. He headed toward it and the others followed. As he got closer, he realized it was a skull. They stopped beneath it.

"This is getting worse by the minute," Infinity muttered.

Although it was high above them, the skull was obviously human-like. But it was larger than a human skull, at least twice the mass. Desmond felt an uneasy prickling on his neck and scalp.

Zachariah pointed. "There are more of them."

He was right. Another skull was mounted atop a post about fifty yards away, and more were spaced out along the fence beyond that. The skulls were arranged so that they faced out toward the forested hills beyond.

Desmond looked at Infinity. A scowl and shake of her head indicated she didn't like this any more than he did.

A faint roar rose above the pelting rain. They all turned at once and saw the herd of camels approaching at full speed. And with them were several dozen riders.

5

———————

HOMINIDS

August 25 - 7:35 AM

THE SITUATION DEFIED Infinity's instinctive impulses. The hominids were coming at them hard, waving what were obviously bows and other weapons. She needed to get the tourists out of harm's way. But the tourists needed to know if the hominids were capable of being friendly or even helpful. From the looks of them at this moment, friendly and helpful were unlikely.

Infinity turned to the fence. It wouldn't be hard to climb this side, but getting down the far side would be a bitch. And so, against her intuition, she said, "Raise your hands above your heads! Do nothing to scare them or make them mad. Don't frown, look at them funny, or yell. Be the most docile, cooperative creatures they've ever seen. Got it?"

Desmond nodded.

"Got it," Zachariah said.

"I'll try," Lorissa said.

And then the camels and riders were upon them. Again, the

riderless camels gathered around, their slobbering lips flapping open and shut. But it was the human-like creatures Infinity was worried about. One of them called out in its high voice. When the gathering of camels didn't budge, several of the hominids urged their mounts forward, forcing the riderless camels to disperse. Infinity, Desmond, and the two tourists were suddenly face to face with the human-like creatures.

"Get your hands up," she reminded the others.

Naked, hairless, and soaking wet, they stood there in the rain. The next seconds would be life or death.

The small beings stared at the humans while the camels beneath them restlessly shuffled back and forth. The hominids were even smaller than Infinity had thought from a distance, probably half her weight or less. They wore knee-length shorts made of brightly-colored cloth. Other than leather moccasins held on with cords tied around their ankles, they wore no other clothing. But each creature had copper bands around its arms and ankles and several copper doodads hanging from its neck. The only hair visible was a tightly-kinked mat of black covering their scalps, and their skin was a light bronze color.

The creatures hadn't yet attacked, but they were certainly equipped to. Each of them carried at least one weapon. Perhaps five of them had a short, thick bow that looked capable of high-velocity shots. Some of them carried a mace-like weapon, but instead of a solid hammer, the copper business end had flat, elongated blades protruding in four directions. Each blade had sawtooth-like points. Those that didn't carry a mace or bow held an axe with a wooden handle and copper blade. About half the creatures were female, and the females wore the same clothing and carried the same weapons as the men. Based on this fact alone, Infinity decided she'd give these creatures the benefit of the doubt, at least until they decided to attack.

She watched their faces, trying to read their intent. Like the rest of their bodies, their round faces were small, only half the size of a human face. With their large, round eyes, these creatures reminded Infinity of a doll she had once found on a playground, the only doll she'd ever owned.

She hoped she didn't have to kill very many of these small people.

The hominids started talking to each other, their voices scratchy but still high, like a child with a sore throat. Their language was filled with wavering and twittering sounds, unlike any language Infinity had heard on previous excursions. It almost sounded like they were singing to each other.

"My arms are getting tired," the tourist, Zachariah, said. "Can I put them down now?"

Before Infinity could answer, Desmond said. "We'll wait until we know it's safe. So suck it up."

Not a bad answer.

Several of the hominids commanded their camels to kneel, and they climbed off without taking their eyes off Infinity's group. When they stood up, they were the height of her belly button, just over three feet.

One of them, a male, approached the humans. Several of the others still mounted on their camels drew back their bows, apparently as a threat in case the humans tried to harm the tiny man. He stopped several feet away and stared, his eyes roaming over their naked bodies.

He spoke. "*Nee-a-na-na-na. Yah-nee-nee-nee.*" There was a flutter within each of the sounds, again reminding Infinity of a singing child.

She glanced over at Desmond. He had surprised her on their previous excursion with his ability to exactly recall sequences of sounds. Apparently he had extraordinary memory for certain things. Desmond nodded, turned to the small man, and repeated the same sounds back, although his deeper voice made them difficult to match.

The small man looked over his shoulder at his companions. The nearest one, a female, skirted around the group and began climbing the fence next to the support post with the weathered skull at the top. When she reached the skull, she pried it off. Holding it in one hand by sticking her fingers in the spinal cord opening at its base, she brought it back down. She carried it to the man who had approached the humans and held it out. The skull was obviously from a human-like creature, but it was much larger than a human skull. Next to these miniature people, it looked even larger. At least four of their heads could fit in the space taken up by this single skull.

The man looked at the skull and looked at the humans. He spoke to the woman and she cautiously approached Desmond, who was closest to her. She raised the skull up, holding it as close to Desmond's head as she could.

Desmond leaned down to where his head was beside it. The skull was about four inches taller and wider than his. "You're right," he said to the tiny woman in a gentle, non-threatening voice. "It's too big. We're not the same species as your enemy. We're not here to hurt you."

Desmond's assumption that the creatures with massive skulls were the enemy of these people was probably correct. But Infinity had a habit of looking at all possible threats. These small people might hunt the larger creatures for sport or food. In which case her group was probably in serious trouble. She decided to watch for an opportunity to demonstrate that the humans could be useful, or perhaps too dangerous to try to kill. Although, based on the size of the skulls mounted on the fence, these tiny people were proficient at killing creatures much larger than themselves.

The hominids began jabbering to each other, including those still mounted on their camels. Twittering, singsong phrases came from all directions, a confusing but also mesmerizing conversation. This was probably the critical moment—they were deciding what to do with the strange new creatures that had appeared in their pasture.

"*Homo floresiensis*," Zachariah said. "Or something close to it. *Floresiensis* were only about as tall as these guys."

"Hardly possible," Desmond replied. "*Homo floresiensis* have been found only on one island in Indonesia."

"But they were capable of getting to that island in the first place, weren't they? Is it unreasonable to think they could have flourished in the last 210,000 years and traveled by boat to North America? Maybe on this version of Earth they spread out to every continent and became the dominant hominid worldwide. These things obviously have metallurgy, at least with copper." Zachariah nudged Desmond's arm. "I think we should call them halflings. That sounds appropriate, don't you think?"

Desmond said, "They're only a third of our mass. Perhaps we should call them thirdlings."

Zachariah nodded his approval.

Impatient, Infinity grunted in disgust. "This is what you guys want to talk about now when these things are deciding if they're going to kill us?"

Zachariah gazed at the small people—the thirdlings—and shook his head. "They look friendly enough to me. I think as long as we—"

He was cut off by a sudden uneasy braying and stamping of hooves from the camels. One of the thirdlings let out a long, wavering cry and pointed to the fence. They all turned to look. Infinity saw them immediately—two creatures standing upright, peering through the gaps between the wood slats. It was hard to see details, but the creatures looked large, even though they were hunched over.

One of them stuck its hand through a gap in the slats, pointing toward Infinity and the other humans. A growling scream rose from its throat, which was joined by a similar scream from the other creature beside it. The two went into a rage, pounding the fence and jumping up and down, all the while grunting and screaming.

Infinity looked at the thirdlings to gauge their reaction. Three of the riders with bows guided their camels over to the fence. They yelled at the creatures and nocked their arrows like they were preparing to fire at them through the slats. This seemed to enrage the creatures even more, and again they pointed through the fence at the humans.

"My God," Lorissa said. "What if we had bridged to the other side of that fence?"

"They're hominids, too," Zachariah said. "But I can't imagine which species they descended from. They're enormous."

The two screaming creatures were joined by three more, probably drawn by the ruckus. The newcomers spotted the humans through the fence and joined their companions in showing raw fury. One of them started climbing the fence. The thirdlings yelled again, but the creature ignored them. One thirdling shot at it. The arrow drilled into one of the wood slats and stopped. Another guided his camel to within a few feet of the fence and shot an arrow through the slats. The climbing creature paused and screamed even louder. But then it kept climbing. It was coming over the fence.

Mounted thirdlings waited for it to clear the top, their bows ready. There was little chance the larger creature could make it over the fence and to the ground alive, but it kept coming anyway, growling and spitting. It forced its way through the spike-riddled lip of the fence and managed to get its head over the top.

Infinity watched the infuriated creature as it stared down at her. It was similar to the neanderthal descendants she had encountered several excursions back, but more than twice the size.

She then realized this creature might offer an opportunity to show the thirdlings that she and her companions could be useful.

The thirdlings with bows were taking aim at the creature, waiting for it to pull its body up into full view. She had to act now.

She raised her arms. "Wait! Don't kill it." Cautiously, she stepped to the nearest thirdling and pointed at the bladed mace in the little woman's hand. In spite of her small size, her mace was plenty large enough to suit Infinity's purpose. "Can I please borrow it?" She asked in the friendliest voice she could manage.

The huge creature was emerging from the spikes onto the top of the fence. The mounted thirdlings were ready to shoot it, but they seemed interested in what Infinity was doing.

"Please, I swear I'll give it back." She held her hand out and curled her fingers twice.

One of the other thirdlings spoke, and the woman before her handed over her weapon.

Infinity smiled at her, although she had no idea what smiling meant to these people.

"Are you crazy?" Desmond asked.

She ignored him and darted over to the fence as the massive creature swung its legs over the top. She held her arms up to the thirdlings with bows. "Please don't shoot!"

Her plan was to surprise the giant just as its feet touched the ground. But as she turned back to the fence, the creature released its grip and dropped ten feet. It hit the ground facing her, snarling and enraged. Her chance for surprise had vanished.

Without hesitating, the massive creature charged her. She had no time to do anything but drop down and to the side to avoid being tackled. As she rolled away, she swiped at its leg with the mace. The weapon was nearly pulled from her grip as one of the serrated blades caught skin like a fish hook and then ripped through it.

The surprised creature stopped and spun around to face her again. Instead of immediately charging, it paused to study her—a sign of intelligence. Or perhaps it was just startled by its new wound.

The creature was brown-skinned, with more body hair than the thirdlings, although Infinity had seen human men far hairier than this. It wore shorts made of animal leather—covering just enough to protect its vulnerable crotch. Brown hair grew loose and unkempt from its scalp, but it had no facial hair. Its massive head was heavy and brutish, with a thick neck. Infinity had fought a number of different hominid opponents, but none as beefy and fierce as this. Luckily, it was injured. The arrow that had been shot through the fence protruded from the middle of its chest. It was bleeding in several places from the fence spikes, and now it had a nasty gash on its lower leg.

Infinity glanced at the thirdlings. They were ready to shoot the creature at any moment, although their small arrows might not kill it before it wreaked some serious havoc.

The giant's companions were still growling as they watched through the fence, apparently not as eager to climb over.

The creature crouched, ready to lunge. Infinity envisioned several possible moves, but she would have to be quick. This was not an opponent she could take to the ground and grapple with. It could probably crush her skull between its hands. The question was, would it fight like an animal or like a human?

It came at her, surprisingly fast for its size.

In a fraction of a second, Infinity read its movements and chose a move. The creature barreled straight for her face, like an animal would. There was no grace or strategy.

So Infinity attacked the way a matador would attack a bull. She left her head and torso—the beast's target—in place until the last possible moment. Instead of risking repeating the same roll-away move, she leapt upward and to the side. As expected, the creature tried to grab her as its momentum carried it past. She brought the mace down on its forearm, a solid slashing blow.

The creature spun around and immediately charged again, howling with rage or pain. This time she went back to her original roll-away move and slashed the creature's ankle from behind, hoping to damage its Achilles tendon. Again, the weapon was nearly torn from her grip.

The giant howled even louder and went down. It tried getting up, but apparently the tendon was severed. Screaming and spitting, it scrambled toward Infinity. It was still dangerous, but now Infinity definitely had the advantage. She shot to her left and then rushed in and landed a blow to the side of its head, opening up a ten-inch gash and mangling its ear.

The creature screamed again and grasped its head. Infinity took this opportunity and landed two more blows to its head. She jumped back just as it swiped at her wildly. Puzzled, she took a moment to glance down at the mace in her hand. Its blades were sharp, and it was reasonably heavy. Those last few blows should have cracked or cut open the creature's skull. But still it struggled to come at her.

One of her hits had apparently destroyed its left eye, so she stayed to its left, circling behind every time it tried to turn far enough to see her. She rushed in again and hit its skull two more times.

This time, the creature stopped screaming, which caused its companions at the fence to go into a heightened fury.

On all fours, it continued turning to its left, but its movements were slower, less coordinated.

Infinity darted in to put it out of its misery. She hit the crown of its skull as hard as she could, embedding one of the mace's blades in the bone. She yanked the blade out as the creature collapsed onto its face.

And then it grabbed her ankle and pulled her off her feet. Its other hand gripped her knee and pulled her closer. It was going for her head.

Infinity kicked its bloody face with her free foot, but it was like kicking a head made of stone.

A shape appeared beside her, and then she heard a solid *thunk*. The creature relaxed its grip on her leg.

Desmond pulled free the mace he had just buried in the giant's forehead. He held a hand out to her.

She gripped it and got to her feet.

"It looked like you needed some help, so I borrowed this." he said, staring at the weapon in his hand. "I can't believe I just killed a human being."

"You'll get over it," she said. But her own hands were shaking, so she crossed her arms to hide it. Then she realized things had become quiet. The rain had stopped. The dead giant's friends at the fence had fallen silent, although they were still staring through the gaps. Lorissa and Zachariah were studying Infinity the way most tourists did after witnessing the raw brutality needed to keep them alive. "You'll get over it, too," she said to them.

Several thirdlings gathered around the giant's corpse, prodding it to make sure it was dead. A tiny hand, palm up, appeared before Infinity. It was the woman who'd loaned her the mace.

"Thank you," Infinity said as she handed the weapon back.

The woman actually smiled, although the roundness of her face and large size of her eyes made the expression slightly terrifying. She gazed up and down Infinity's body. She then extended her free hand and touched Infinity's knee. She sang, "*Walah-ree-ro-ro-ro.*"

Infinity realized her leg had been smeared with the giant's blood where it had tried to pull her closer. "It's not my blood," she said. "It's his." She pointed to the body.

Another female thirdling approached and also touched Infinity's leg. She sang another brief statement.

Infinity looked down and realized the women were referring to a ragged scratch just below the knee, probably from the giant's fingernails. "It's nothing serious," she said, although she knew that in a world without antibiotics, a scratch could be fatal.

The two thirdling women sang to each other, loud enough for

the other thirdlings to hear. This was followed by a verbal exchange among all of them.

Finally, the two women smiled at Infinity and pointed to something in the distance. She looked. They were pointing to the rounded rooftops and rising columns of black smoke. The women took a few steps and gestured for Infinity and the others to follow.

Surrounded by a herd of camels, some carrying tiny riders, the four humans walked barefoot and naked toward the thirdling village.

6

COPPER

August 25 - 8:22 AM

As they moved away from the scene of the fight, Desmond turned to look back. The four remaining giants still watched from behind the fence, their angry calls now fading. The hominid's body, now just a dark lump in the grassy pasture, had been left where it had died.

Riderless camels crowded Desmond as he walked, popping their lips and occasionally smearing goo on his shoulders and neck. It was as if they were fascinated by a species of human they had never seen or smelled before.

"I guess the thirdlings aren't interested in butchering the big one for meat." Infinity said. "That's a good sign."

Desmond considered this and decided it was a *very* good sign.

Zachariah was busy trying to avoid the flapping camel lips, but he spoke up. "If we're going to call the small ones thirdlings, it seems only fitting to call the large ones orcs or goblins. I do believe Tolkien would approve."

Desmond glanced over at the parasitologist and smiled. The guy was nerdy but likable.

Zachariah noticed and smiled back. "Did you know there's only one thing worse than a mecium? A paramecium."

Desmond snorted a laugh. Yes, definitely nerdy. "Zach, did I hear you actually say 'Heavens to Betsy' as we were being charged by a herd of camels?"

"They say danger reveals one's true nature," he replied. "I suppose 'Heavens to Betsy' sums me up pretty well."

"Perhaps you could put your intellect to better use," Lorissa said with a disapproving tone. "Seven hundred people are counting on us."

Zachariah shrugged. "I'm pretty much useless here. It's impossible to evaluate microbiotic factors without lab equipment and the time to use it properly. So my role has changed. I'm now the cheerleader for this team. Perhaps, Lorissa, you could share your assessment of what you've so far witnessed?"

She glared at him. "Well, there is obviously a flourishing animal husbandry tradition among these hominids."

"Thirdlings," Zachariah said.

She frowned. "Whatever. I have yet to see plant crops, but the soil certainly is suitable. If we determine that these thirdlings are willing to help our colony get established, well, I can't imagine we could ask for a better scenario."

They came to another fence, also made of timber but much lower than the outer fence. It was the height of Desmond's chest, just enough to contain the camels. They passed through a gate with copper hinges. Several thirdlings sang and whistled to prevent the riderless camels from crowding through the gate while the humans and mounted thirdlings passed through. Outside the gate was a road with two worn tracks about four feet apart. On the far side of the road, between their position and the thirdling village, was another fenced pasture.

A herd of several hundred cow-sized mammals came running and gathered at the fence, as if waiting to be fed. At first, Desmond thought they might be some kind of thickly-furred boar, but then he saw one open its mouth, revealing four massive incisors. The creatures were rodents. They somewhat resembled the capybara of Desmond's world, only much larger—easily 1,000 pounds each. Their brown fur was broken up by diagonal white stripes from the shoulders back to the rump. The creatures hummed and squealed at the group passing by on the road, like amplified, baritone guinea pigs.

They came to a four-way intersection. Each road was straight and was lined on both sides by the fences of additional livestock pastures. In the distance, Desmond saw a mass of black animals unlike the camels or rodents, but they were too far away to identify. The thirdlings turned right onto a road leading directly to the village.

As they approached the domed structures, the air became pungent with an acidic, sulfurous odor.

"Smell that?" Zachariah asked. "Copper smelting. It has to be. Which explains the prevalence of their copper ornamentation and weapons."

Another dozen or so thirdlings on camels rode out to meet them, resulting in several minutes of singsong conversation as they apparently talked about the humans.

They proceeded onward, only to be joined by more riders, and then more after that. Soon the mass of escorts was stretched out ahead and behind.

It became evident that the dome-roofed structures were situated in the center of a vast array of roads and fenced pastures. At least a hundred thirdlings were gathered around as they passed the last livestock enclosure and entered the village itself. There were children here, between two and three feet tall. Every thirdling wore knee-length shorts, the only difference being wildly-varying colors.

Copper ornamentation was standard, and Desmond noticed a fish-shaped piece of copper hung from the neck of every citizen, including the kids. From what he could see, there were no differences between the clothing, ornaments, or hair of males and females. The only detectable difference was the presence of tiny, bulbous breasts on the females. In fact, their behavior was also indistinguishable, which perhaps meant their social roles were similar.

For what seemed like more than an hour, Desmond and his companions were forced to stand in the road while the thirdlings chattered to each other and stared. He tried counting them, and although their restless moving made this difficult, he estimated 150. Based on the number of houses and other structures he could see, this was possibly the entire population.

A male thirdling emerged from the crowd, carrying an armload of green fabric. Moving with purpose, he stopped in front of each human and handed over a piece of the fabric. Desmond accepted his and held it open with both hands. It was a pair of shorts, similar to those worn by the hominids but larger. The tiny man pointed to Desmond's groin and then smiled, displaying relatively white teeth with one-inch canines. Perhaps this species was more adapted than *Homo sapiens* to eating flesh.

"I guess they're not comfortable with us being in our birthday suits," Zachariah said. "I'm impressed they made these so quickly."

The pants were larger than any of the thirdlings could possibly wear, so the garments must have been cut and sewn in the minutes since the humans had arrived.

They all pulled on their shorts. Two long pieces of the cloth extended from the front, and it was clear from observing the thirdlings' shorts that these were to be tied together to cinch the shorts tight. The fabric was soft and the knee-length pants were reasonably comfortable.

Many of the thirdlings suddenly raised their arms over their heads, their hands quivering like leaves in the wind. They called out, "*Loo-roh-roh-roh.*" Desmond sensed that they were expressing delight that the humans had put on the pants, although the display could have meant something completely different.

"We're the only ones here with green shorts." Infinity said. "Any ideas why?"

She was obviously uneasy about this. Not surprising, since Infinity looked for potential danger in just about everything.

"Maybe the colors represent something to these people," he said. "Maybe social castes, or something like that. We're obviously different from them, so we get green."

Infinity finished tying her shorts around her waist. "Something else I'd like to know—who created all this? They have metal and good fabric and impressive fences. But they're too damn small. Their brains can't be more than a third the size of ours."

Desmond knew what she was thinking—that another more intelligent, more dangerous species could be involved. This is what she and Desmond had seen in the bird people on their last excursion.

"These hominids are approximately the size of *Homo flore-siensis*," Zachariah said. "But in spite of diminutive brains, *flore-siensis* used tools and fire. And I should point out that it's likely these thirdlings have evolved from a larger ancestor. In hominids, a gradually reducing brain size may not equate to diminished intellect. If they descended from *Homo erectus*, for example, it is quite possible their brains underwent what is referred to as neurological reorganization. In which case the functions of the brain were maintained, even as it became smaller."

Desmond appraised him. "I thought you were a microbiologist."

"All that matters," Lorissa interjected, "is that our colony will thrive here. Zachariah may be a microbiologist, but I'm an agricultural specialist, and I see great potential in the existing agricultural infrastructure here. I don't care how intelligent these things are, as long as they'll help us. Once we get established, maybe we can have them work our fields for us. Or they can protect us from those gremlins."

"Goblins," Zachariah said. "Or orcs. But not gremlins."

Desmond gazed at Lorissa for a moment, not sure what to think of her statement. For the sake of the refugees in her colony—and for the thirdlings—he hoped she wouldn't be chosen as the colony's leader.

They were taken into the village. White, dome-roofed dwellings stood on either side of the narrow unpaved road. Most were cottage-sized by Desmond's perspective, but even the smallest structures were probably large enough to house up to ten thirdlings. Instead of rectangular, the structures were round or oval. Such a shape would be difficult to construct if using logs or boards. But since the outer walls and roofs were covered in dried and painted mud or concrete of some kind, perhaps wood wasn't a major structural component. Spaced every few feet around the walls were narrow, vertical openings. They were probably for ventilation, but they resembled the arrow slits of a castle. Small, tight-fitting doors appeared to be made of smooth copper. In the center of each domed roof was a single chimney. From a distance, each structure looked like a short white cylinder with half of a ping pong ball mounted on top. They were symmetrical, with smooth surfaces, indicating sophisticated engineering and craftsmanship. Desmond estimated there were about forty of these structures in the village.

The areas around the structures, as well as the roads, were tidy and manicured, although there were no cultivated plants or grasses to be seen anywhere. Everything was bare gravel and white walls. Apparently camels weren't allowed into this part of the village. They had been left at the village perimeter near the pasture fences. No other non-thirdling animals, such as dogs, were evident. Perhaps dogs didn't even exist on this world.

They passed a domed structure that was larger than most of the others. Black smoke billowed from several chimneys, and here the acrid smell of sulfur was even stronger.

"This has to be a copper smelting facility," Zachariah muttered, possibly talking to himself. Then louder, he said, "These thirdlings are smarter than they appear. That sulfurous odor is sulfur dioxide."

"What's your point?" Lorissa asked.

He shook his head as if she should already know his point. "Sulfur dioxide results from burning copper sulfide—copper ore. This means these humans have probably long-ago exhausted the supply of pure native copper at the surface of this world. After that, they would have figured out the simplest copper smelting technique, which is the charcoal reduction of oxidic minerals of copper. But then they must have exhausted the supply of oxidic copper ores." He paused. "I'm sure you're anxious to know how I deduce that?"

They all just stared at him.

He went on. "Burning copper sulfide is part of a much more complex smelting technique, and the thirdlings wouldn't be doing it unless they had exhausted the native copper and the oxidic ores. The next logical approach is what is called matte smelting, a multistep technique that first involves burning copper sulfide. Hence the smell of sulfur dioxide." He smiled at them, obviously pleased with the chance to share his knowledge.

"My point is, though, that matte smelting is complex. And just producing the necessary high temperatures is a challenge. But these thirdlings have figured it out. This is proof that their brains are quite analytical, in spite of the smaller size. I would go as far as to suggest they might be as intelligent as we are, although not as far along in progressing through the industrial and technological spectrum."

"Which means they're dangerous as hell," Infinity said. "We need to be ready for anything, so stay alert."

Stopped on the side of the road next to the smelting structure was a wagon hitched to two camels, the only camels they'd seen within the perimeter of the cluster of buildings. At first, Desmond hadn't realized they were actually camels, because other than their legs, they were covered in articulated copper armor. And the enclosed wagon itself was fortified with armor. Two female thirdlings sat atop the wagon, staring at the humans and their numerous escorts as they walked by. The women held short, thick bows in their laps, and a supply of arrows bristled from a cylindrical copper quiver between them. Desmond noticed the copper ornaments hanging from their necks were spirals, unlike the fish-shaped ornaments he'd seen so far. Perhaps these women were traders from another village. But he didn't have much time to consider this because the mass of thirdlings didn't slow down, and he and his companions were swept along with them.

They approached a low, circular building Desmond guessed was near the center of the village. Like the other structures, vertical slits were arranged around the outer wall about two feet apart. But this building was larger than the others. In fact, if Desmond's estimate of 150 for the village population was correct, this building could probably accommodate all of them at once.

The humans were led to a low entrance with a door that appeared to be solid copper. Constructed for thirdlings, the doorway was no more than four and a half feet high, and they had to bend over to pass through. Desmond noted the structure's outer wall was several feet thick, and the door itself appeared to be heavily fortified.

Surprisingly, the interior was cool, although it was a warm August morning. This was perhaps due to the structure's thick wall and white exterior. It was darker inside, but the wall slits allowed in plenty of light. And it helped that the interior wall and ceiling were also white.

"My God, they brought us to an armory," Zachariah said.

He was right. The interior was one large circular room, and spaced evenly around the perimeter between the slits were racks of weapons. Particularly bows—hundreds of them—and thousands of arrows protruding from upright tubular containers. There were copper-bladed axes, and maces with blades like the one Desmond had used to finish off the giant orc. And several long spears were propped against the wall next to each window slit.

"It's not an armory," Infinity said. "It's a redoubt."

Desmond frowned at her. "A redoubt?"

"A stronghold. Think about it. They have a fortified outer fence. Even their livestock is within that fence. It's not easy, but those giant hominids—the orcs—can get over the fence if they're motivated enough. This structure is a last-resort stronghold. It's big enough to hold the entire population, and it's built to withstand an onslaught from hell. They even have supplies." She waved toward the center of the chamber. Stacked there were dozens of copper boxes. Next to the boxes were wood-strip barrels with copper hoops, remarkably similar to the whisky barrels still being used back on their own world.

The vertical slits in the outer walls of the houses looked like arrow slits because that's exactly what they were. The entire thirdling village was designed to be defensible.

Perhaps a hundred thirdlings crowded into the stronghold, apparently interested in what would happen next. The situation was unnerving, but Desmond had relaxed some since entering the village. If the thirdlings planned on killing them, why would they bother giving them specially-designed pants?

For the next few hours, the thirdlings stood in a circle around the humans and chattered to each other. There was no furniture, so Desmond and the others finally sat on the floor. Every few minutes, one of the thirdlings would step forward and try speaking to them. Desmond did his best to repeat back the sequences of sounds. At first, this excited the little hominids, until they realized he was just parroting and had no idea what it meant. The thirdlings tried gesturing with their hands, but it soon became obvious they had developed different conventions for this type of symbolism. Very little of it made sense.

Four thirdlings entered the stronghold and pushed their way through the throng. Each of them held a copper cup and plate, which they placed on the floor before the humans. The cups contained a dark liquid. Each plate contained nothing but meat. The meat was in two piles, one that was raw, and one that was obviously freshly cooked—it was still steaming.

Desmond eyed Infinity. Normally she would order them to avoid eating and drinking during an excursion. The water and food could be toxic due to different biological processes that may have evolved since the world diverged from their own version of Earth. But the game had changed. Zachariah and Lorissa were here to assess this world's viability for a human colony.

Infinity opened her mouth to speak, but Zachariah beat her to it. "Without lab equipment, there's no way to determine how this will affect our physiology, other than to simply consume it."

Infinity nodded. "I agree. Desmond and I will eat and drink. But not you two. If it kills us, you'll still be able to bridge back and tell the others what happened here."

"I disagree," Lorissa said. "You told us we'll bridge back no matter what happens to us. Even if we're dead. Our returning bodies will tell all that needs to be told. I'm responsible for an entire colony. You do what you want, but I need first-hand proof that this world is suitable."

Infinity glared at her, and Desmond knew she was struggling with this dilemma. She was hard-wired to do anything to keep tourists alive until bridge-back. But things were different now.

Finally, she sighed. "Suit yourself." She reached for her copper cup and sniffed its contents. She frowned and put it back down. "It's alcoholic."

Infinity had told Desmond weeks before that she never touched alcohol. 'Why would I dump shit into my body?' she had said.

The two scientists drank from their cups. They both nodded their approval.

Desmond took a sip. The liquid was like a flat stout, with little or no carbonation. But it wasn't unpleasant. His portion of meat that was cooked smelled pretty good. Blood from the raw meat was trickling into the cooked meat, so he tipped the plate to stop it. He pulled a chunk of the cooked meat loose and found it to be lightly spiced and tender. As he ate it, the thirdlings again raised their hands and shook them back and forth, shouting "*Loo-roh-roh-roh.*" Apparently they were easy to please.

Soon the cooked portions of meat had all been eaten, and—except for Infinity's—the stout was gone. The drink was strong enough that Desmond felt pleasantly euphoric.

A female thirdling stepped between Desmond and Infinity from behind. She held a small copper dish containing a lump of greenish paste. She pointed to the scratch on Infinity's leg and then scooped the paste onto her fingers and smeared it onto the ragged, six-inch abrasion. Infinity allowed this without protesting, perhaps because everything about the gesture suggested the thirdling was generously attempting to treat the wound.

Another female thirdling came forward and placed two objects on the floor that could only be described as books. They were rectangular but long, perhaps five inches by three feet. Along one of the long edges were numerous copper rings binding together two thick rectangles of stiff leather. The woman arranged one of them so that the copper rings were facing away from the humans and pulled the top leather cover open, revealing the first in a pile of off-white pages. The pages were of some type of smooth paper or fine fabric. Arranged on the long page from left to right—or perhaps right to left—were drawings.

Zachariah immediately moved his cup and plate aside and

crowded forward to inspect the page. "This is fascinating!" He lifted the page to reveal the next page, which contained more drawings. He flipped through the remaining pages. "They have intricate artwork, but I see no written words. They smelt copper ore, but they don't have a written language?"

"Maybe the pictures *are* their language," Desmond said. "Or maybe it's just a simple picture book, because they know we couldn't read their words anyway." He scooted forward on his butt to look more closely at the drawings. Many of the pictures were obviously of people—thirdlings probably—engaged in various activities. The drawn figures were stylized in a strange way, with disproportionately-large heads, feet, and hands, as well as oversized breasts on the females. But there was no doubt what they were. There were images of people with camels and other animals, and of people apparently constructing fences, houses, and a variety of unidentifiable things. There were groups of people gathered together in various arrangements, perhaps social events. Desmond flipped through the pages. Several pages down were drawings of thirdlings together with much larger people—orcs, probably. He gazed at each of these images and then flipped the page. There were more, and more on the page after that. And every one of the images depicted fighting and killing. Beyond a doubt, the thirdlings and orcs were mortal enemies.

"I can't help but be excited about this," Lorissa said. "At every turn, these people have welcomed us. They've given us clothing, fed us, treated Infinity's wound, and now they're teaching us about their culture. This is it, Zachariah. This is the permanent home for our colony!"

Desmond watched Infinity's reaction to this. She was staring at the drawings, frowning.

He turned back to the book and flipped to the next page. Something here caught his eye and he leaned in to look closer. The first drawing on the left showed two thirdlings pointing their bows at a much larger orc. But beside the thirdlings was another human-like figure that was larger than the thirdlings but smaller than the orc. He looked at the next drawing. Again there were two thirdlings and a figure of intermediate size. They were side-by-side, standing over a dead orc. The last two drawings on the page also showed all three species. In each one, the thirdlings stood to the side while the intermediate figure was apparently chopping up the orc's body.

"Are you seeing this?" Desmond asked the others.

"Infinity put her finger on the intermediate figure on one of the drawings. "This is why the orcs went ballistic when they saw us through the perimeter fence."

"It's a third species," Zachariah said. "And from the looks of this, the third species may be friends with the thirdlings."

"And they kill orcs," Desmond added.

"They may be *Homo sapiens*," Lorissa said. "This is good news, right?"

"That's never good news," Infinity said.

Zachariah pointed. "Look at these drawings. What do you see that's different about them?"

Desmond looked. He hadn't paid attention to it before, but the drawings were specked with dots, maybe rain falling. But the ground was different as well. In fact, on the previous drawings, the thirdlings hadn't even bothered drawing the ground at all. "It's snow," he said. He flipped to the next page. There were more draw-ings with all three hominid sizes. And in each one, the orcs were being attacked or butchered—in a snow storm.

"These images reveal a great deal, and the thirdlings have a knack for including pertinent details," Zachariah said. "I do believe this third species—possibly *Homo sapiens*—may be friendly to the thirdlings. And it appears they come here in the winter to kill orcs. Which would explain why we have yet to see them."

Desmond was beginning to appreciate Zachariah's deductive

mind. Winter could certainly be when a hominid species might expand its hunting range due to the scarcity of game.

He turned to the tiny woman and pointed to the second book beside her. "Can I see that one?"

She slid it closer to him and then sat cross-legged beside it. She opened it, revealing a blank page. Another woman handed her something that Desmond recognized immediately. It was a small copper ink pot holding a copper quill pen.

She spoke to Desmond in her lyrical language and with exaggerated motions pulled the quill pen out, tapped it to shed excess ink, and drew on the page. First, she drew a female person, in the same style as the other drawings. Then beside it she drew a larger person, and then another. Soon there were four, two of them with exaggerated breasts, the other two with oversized penises. She sat back and studied Desmond. Her round, weathered face, with its large eyes and nearly absent forehead, was expressive. These people were attractive in their own way. As Desmond gazed back at her, she smiled broadly. She then handed him the pen and slid the ink pot in his direction.

Desmond glanced at his companions.

"First contact with another intelligent species," Zachariah said. He then huffed a laugh. "Don't screw it up."

The thirdlings crowded around and watched quietly, expectantly.

Desmond turned back to the diminutive woman. He sighed. There was one big thing, above all else, that he needed to communicate to these people. He dipped the pen, tapped it on the pot's rim, and flipped the page, revealing a blank sheet.

Trying to mimic the thirdlings' distinctive style, on the left end of the page he drew a figure standing beside a dome-roofed dwelling with arrow-slit windows. To the right of it he drew a larger figure, one with a penis. He extended the larger figure's arm so that its hand touched the hand of the thirdling beside it, and he attempted to draw smiles on the two faces. He drew three more of the larger figures, one man and two women. He then glanced up at the thirdling before him, hoping to signify the importance of what he would do next. She was watching intently.

To the right of the four nude humans, he drew another human. And then another. He continued drawing humans, spreading them out to fill up the length of the rectangular page, and then he added more by overlaying them on top of those he'd already drawn. He moved his hand faster, becoming less concerned about detail, just to get more humans on the page. Finally, he stopped before the figures became so crowded they weren't recognizable. He turned the book around and pushed it closer to the woman.

She picked it up, got to her feet, and moved to the other thirdlings. They gathered around her, singing to each other in their melodic, otherworldly language.

7

———————

LORISSA

August 25 - 7:07 PM

A BRIDGER's job was to keep tourists alive until bridge-back. That's how it had always been, and Infinity had been a bridger from the beginning. Four years—longer than anyone. The job wasn't about making friends with the natives. Because no matter how goddamn cute or interesting the natives were, they were always trouble. No exceptions, at least none Infinity had seen. Until maybe now.

Throughout the day, the thirdlings had shown again and again that they intended no harm to the humans. Twice they had provided food and drink, although Infinity had gone to some trouble trying to convince them she wanted only water. She never did get water, but finally they brought her some sweet pink juice that was nonalcoholic.

The thirdlings had brought out book after boring book of pictures, pointing and talking as if they believed the humans would finally understand if they heard the words a thousand times.

For several hours, the thirdlings demonstrated some kind of

dance. Or maybe it was a game, or even a form of talking—who the hell knew? They got Desmond and the tourist, Zachariah, to get up and try some of the moves. The thirdlings didn't seem to laugh the same way humans did, but Infinity was pretty sure they thought that was funny. Wretched was what it was.

Finally, the thirdlings had led them out of the stronghold and to a smaller house, which was where they were now. And apparently they were expected to spend the night there. Only about twenty thirdlings were still present, and every one of them was armed with a copper-bladed mace and a bow. Wisely, they didn't fully trust the larger humans.

Infinity had gradually become convinced the thirdlings didn't intend to kill them. But still she was uneasy. Seven hundred and eighteen lives were at stake, which was 715 more than she had ever had to protect on an excursion.

"We need to talk about the situation," she said to the others during a rare moment when the remaining thirdlings were occupied with discussing something between themselves. "I'm guessing bridge-back is in about twenty-four hours, at which time we'll have minutes to make a report."

"I can't imagine what there is to talk about," Lorissa said. "The thirdlings have given every indication that they will help us survive here, and—"

Infinity stopped her with a raised hand. "Shut up and hear what I have to say. This is a village of about 150 thirdlings. There's no way in hell your colony of over 700 humans can live here with them, even if the thirdlings wanted you to. I'm sure there are other villages, but we know nothing about them. Even if each village took in fifty humans, that would take fourteen villages."

"And each human is three times the mass of a thirdling," Desmond added. "So fifty humans would double the biomass that the village would have to feed."

"Then we start our own village," Lorissa said.

Infinity stared at her for a moment. Was the woman really this stupid? "Where? In the forest beyond the perimeter fence? With the orcs?"

Lorissa opened her mouth to argue like she was on autopilot. But then she stopped. She blinked away tears that were forming in her eyes. "It has to work. We may not get another chance."

"It takes seventy-two hours to do another bio-probe and an assessment excursion," Infinity said. "You'll get another chance."

Lorissa wiped her cheek and shook her head, but she didn't reply.

"It's the orcs that you fear," Zachariah said. "But what I fear is far more terrifying. These thirdlings are a different species, but they are close enough to us that they almost certainly harbor pathogens that could make the leap. The same could be said for the orcs. Without antibiotics or medical equipment, our entire colony could be wiped out by any of a thousand diseases within the first few months. What we need is a world without hominids at all. Or we need to convince the colony to bridge to a world with a very recent divergence point. Like only one year."

"We've voted on that!" Lorissa sobbed. "They want a world without humans. And with cold weather coming, we don't have the time to try over and over again. This world already has shelters, and fences, and livestock. Maybe it will be *our* pathogens that wipe out the thirdlings, and then we'll be able to use their villages."

Again, Infinity stared at her.

"Jesus, Lorissa," Zachariah said.

As gutsy as it had been for Lorissa to say this, it was true. And Infinity understood the raw survival instinct it took to formulate such a thought. She had killed neanderthals and several other human-like creatures in order to protect human tourists. Hell, she had even killed a few human residents of other worlds. It was better than losing a tourist.

Unfortunately, Lorissa's logic didn't provide good enough odds.

"But there's far less than a 50% chance of that happening," Zachariah pointed out. "Some of our pathogens bridge here with our bodies, but we're relatively sterile when we bridge, due to all the antibiotics we're given in preparation. It's far more likely we'll be on the receiving end of the pathogen deal."

"Then maybe we could inject the colonists with some kind of virus," Lorissa said. "Something we're sure the thirdlings would contract."

Desmond and Zachariah looked dumbfounded. Infinity realized she hadn't really known Lorissa until this moment.

Zachariah shook his head and said, "It wouldn't change anything, because the colony would be just as likely to contract diseases from the thirdlings."

Lorissa's pleading stare was intense. "But it would help, right? I mean, if we get lucky and *don't* contract a deadly disease from the thirdlings, we'll have access to their resources and—"

"It's not happening." Infinity said. "There are rules."

"But surely those rules are no longer valid, considering what's going on."

"I said it's not happening!" Infinity realized her aggressive tone had startled the nearby thirdlings. They were now watching them, their big eyes even rounder than usual. Several of them tightened their grips on their bows and maces.

"Let's not give our hosts a reason to rescind their hospitality," Desmond said calmly. "I think we can all agree this world presents substantial problems for a colony. Do you agree, Lorissa?"

She wiped her cheek again and nodded slightly. But the fierce determination in her eyes remained.

* * *

11:49 PM

· · ·

THE TWO TOURISTS were finally asleep, but Infinity wasn't sure about Desmond. The mattresses they'd been given—cases of fine fabric stuffed with what might have been camel hair—were soft, but she shifted her body and let out a grunt as if she were uncomfortable.

"Can't sleep?" Desmond asked. His mattress was inches from hers, so his whispered words were clear.

She smiled into the darkness. "Sleeping usually isn't an option on excursions, in spite of what happened to me last time."

She heard him reach out for her. His fingers came in contact with her breast. He quickly realized what he was touching and moved his hand to her stomach. She smiled again. They hadn't made love yet, but she thought about it sometimes. With all the crap that was going on, though, it would probably never happen.

"I can't sleep either," he said. "This is a huge responsibility—all those lives at stake."

"Yeah."

"Do you think there's any way they could survive here?"

"Not likely." Actually, there wasn't a chance in hell.

He was quiet for a moment. "Infinity?"

Instead of answering, she put her hand on his.

"I hope when the time comes we can bridge with one of the colonies," he said. "To stay, I mean."

"I know what you mean. Again, not likely." They had talked about this before. She and Desmond had been assigned to assist as many colonies as possible. And they'd been promised that when conditions on Earth got really bad, they could join the last colony and bridge one-way to an alternate world. But she knew this wasn't going to happen. There would always be one more colony waiting to evacuate, up until the moment the bridging center was destroyed by an earthquake or storm. And that would be it.

"But I still hope for it," he said.

She pressed his hand more firmly against her belly.

"No, stop!" It was Lorissa. She could be heard thrashing around in the darkness. "Stop!"

"She's having a nightmare," Desmond whispered. "I can understand why."

Infinity sighed and pushed his hand from her. "I'll wake her, otherwise she'll freak out the thirdlings." The thirdlings had left them alone in the domed house, but guards were almost certainly watching the door from outside. She got to her hands and knees and felt her way to Lorissa's side. She shook the woman's shoulder.

"Stop!" Lorissa sat upright and got to her feet. "No!" She scrambled away and Infinity heard her trip and fall and get up again. "I don't want to!" She fumbled with something and then threw open the door.

Now Infinity could see her shape against the dim light of the open doorway. In a panic, the damn woman bent over and bolted out into the night.

"Stay here!" Infinity shouted to Desmond. She moved to the doorway and ducked through.

Lorissa had already crossed the road and was sprawled on the gravel at the base of another dwelling, sobbing. Several thirdlings stood over her, holding their bows ready to kill her if necessary.

Infinity approached them slowly. "Please don't shoot my friend," she said softly. "She doesn't mean you harm. I'll take her back inside."

The thirdlings glanced back and forth between Lorissa and Infinity, obviously on edge.

Infinity held her hands out. "It's okay. It's okay."

The thirdlings pulled back, allowing her to approach Lorissa.

Kneeling, Infinity put a hand on Lorissa's shoulder. "You okay?"

"No, I'm not okay," she sobbed. "I don't deserve to be here. I don't deserve to be part of a colony."

Infinity glanced up at the waiting thirdlings, but their features were only shadows in the dark. "Of course you do. They selected you because you're qualified."

"You don't know me! You don't know what I've done. No one knows."

Infinity closed her eyes and counted to three. She had no interest in being Lorissa's counselor. "We've all done things we regret. Your colony will be a fresh start for you."

Lorissa was shaking and crying. "I killed my dad!"

Infinity opened her eyes and stared at her. "You what?"

"A few weeks ago. After everyone knew the end was coming. He still lived on our farm in Oregon. I drove out to see him. I don't know why. Maybe I thought I should see him one more time—tell him goodbye. Even though we weren't close. In fact, I hated him. I've always hated him, since I was a little girl."

Infinity really didn't want to hear this. But maybe if Lorissa could spit it all out, she'd calm down.

"I thought I could make amends." Her voice was breaking and pitiful. "Because I don't have other family. That's why I was selected for the colony. So I went to see him. But it didn't work. He was hateful. Just like always. He hated me for being picked. For leaving him behind. For leaving everyone behind. It got ugly. I tried to leave. He grabbed me. Like he used to grab me. So I hit him. With an iron he used as a doorstop. I hit him more than once. Oh, God!" She put her hands over her face.

Infinity could guess what had happened next. "So you left and didn't tell anyone?"

Lorissa nodded behind her hands. "I knew I'd lose my spot in the colony. I just went home. A few days later it was time to go to Missouri. To SafeTrek. I don't want to lose my spot, Infinity. I can't. It's my chance to help people. To make up for what I did."

How the hell was Infinity supposed to deal with this? She took a deep breath, deciding on a course of action. After glancing again at the thirdlings surrounding them, she firmly grabbed Lorissa's ears, forcing the woman to look up at her.

"Do you notice how I'm talking calmly? It's because I don't want these thirdlings to kill us. So the next time you speak, keep that in mind. Listen carefully. I don't care about your dad, and I don't care what you've done. But I care about the people in your colony. And I care about Desmond and Zachariah. Here's the goddamn deal. You're going to stop acting like a psychopathic bitch. Because this is important. If you can act normal until bridge-back, I won't tell Reece Eagleton what you've told me. And you'll still have your spot in the colony. Do you understand?"

Lorissa nodded without speaking.

"I've seen you acting sane, so I know you're capable. Get your shit together or you may not even make it to bridge-back." Infinity released her ears. "Speak calmly and tell me you're going to do that."

Lorissa rubbed her right ear. "I'm going to act sane. You don't have to worry."

Infinity extended a hand to her. "Good. Now get up, walk to the road, and then squat and pee."

"What? Why?"

"Because I want these thirdlings to think you were upset because you needed to pee. You have to go, right?"

"I've had to go for hours." She allowed Infinity to pull her up. She went to the road, pulled down her shorts, and squatted.

"*Me-lee-cree-cree-cree!*" the nearest thirdling cried. She was a female, and she grabbed Lorissa's shorts and pulled them back up. She then led her by the hand back to the dwelling.

When they were inside again, the female thirdling went to the wall and touched something. There was a click, and a small flame ignited inside a lantern mounted three feet up on the wall. The flame was encased in a faded globe that might have been blown glass.

Desmond and Zachariah got up and gathered around as the thirdling went to a flat white disk on the floor, apparently made of the same stuff as the house itself. She shoved the disk aside with her tiny foot, revealing a dark hole about ten inches across. The gentle sound of flowing water could be heard from below the hole—a sewage system.

The thirdling mimicked the act of squatting over the hole, and then she stood to the side, waiting.

"Thank God," Zachariah said, and he rushed over to the hole. "Pardon me, ladies, but this has been a long time coming."

8

CLASS

SOMETHING HAD CHANGED between Infinity and the agriculture scientist, Lorissa. Desmond was sure of that. Lorissa was avoiding eye contact and was keeping to herself more than usual. After Lorissa's waking nightmare and panic attack, they had all slept at least a few hours, and now sunlight was streaming through the window slits on the east side of the dwelling. Thirdlings could be heard talking outside, but so far none had come in to check on them.

Desmond glanced at the others one more time to make sure their backs were turned and hurriedly finished defecating into the hole in the floor. If he hadn't eaten so much of the meat offered by the thirdlings yesterday, he could have avoided this humiliating chore. A soft fabric towel hung beside the latrine, but since Desmond was the last of the four to do this, he had to carefully manipulate it to find an area not already soiled. He hoped this was the intended purpose for the towel, otherwise the thirdlings might be offended by how the fine piece of fabric had been desecrated.

"Okay, you can turn around," he said after using the towel and pulling up his green shorts. Zachariah and Infinity turned, but Lorissa continued staring out through one of the slits.

Desmond gazed at Infinity until he caught her eye, then he nodded toward Lorissa, silently asking what was going on with her. Infinity frowned and shook her head, which probably meant she had an answer but wouldn't discuss it now.

The door swung inward, and three thirdlings stepped in, all of them holding bows with arrows nocked and ready to pull back. After several seconds of uneasy silence, one of them sang a few phrases and more thirdlings came in, bearing plates heaped with cooked meat. They also had copper cups of the dark stout for Desmond, Zachariah, and Lorissa, and pink juice for Infinity.

Zachariah immediately sat on the floor before the plates. "Not that I'm complaining, but what's a guy got to do to get a salad around here?"

"They're carnivores," Infinity replied. "It's even possible this is orc meat."

Zachariah cocked his head and eyed her for a moment with a frown. Then he chuckled. "I thought bridgers were supposed to be helpful." He poked at the contents of one of the plates, selected a fist-sized chunk of the meat, and began eating.

Other than an undeniable need to crap when he had awakened, Desmond had felt no ill effects from the meat, so he also helped himself.

About fifteen thirdlings gathered around and watched as the humans ate their fill. Desmond noticed one of them was the same woman who had communicated with him using drawings. She and at least two of the men seemed to be of some importance in this community. When these individuals talked, the others always fell silent and listened. And these same three had been present each time there was a gathering around the humans. They either had an interest in, or were in charge of, the thirdling-human interactions.

As Desmond ate, he occupied his thoughts with assigning names to the three he was becoming familiar with. The more time he spent with them, the easier it was to tell them apart, although still the only way he could distinguish females from males was by their breasts. The female, he decided, would be Jane, because Calamity Jane was the first person who came to mind. Whether it was true or not, Calamity Jane had a reputation for fighting native Americans. The two men he named Bill and Hickok, because Wild Bill Hickok was the only name he could think of to go along with Calamity Jane.

After collecting the empty cups and plates, the thirdlings guided the humans out the door and onto the road. They then turned and headed east toward the rising sun. By the time they stopped at a large, white-domed structure at the edge of the village, another twenty or so thirdlings had stopped what they were doing to follow the group.

They entered the structure through a door that was wider and taller than those they'd so far seen. Once Desmond was inside, he understood why. The open space within the structure was clearly a training area. Several dozen young thirdlings were gathered around two female adults who appeared to be demonstrating techniques for fighting with the same bladed maces Desmond and Infinity had used to kill the orc the previous day. Beyond the thirdlings, attached to the far wall by thick copper chains, were three hulking figures. Somehow, and for some reason, the thirdlings had brought live orcs here.

Desmond exchanged a glance with Infinity. Her frown indicated she was as disturbed by this as he was.

The instructors paused their lesson as the humans were led around the perimeter of the room. Song-like chattering resonated throughout the chamber as the young thirdlings gathered around.

Jane, Bill, and Hickok paused to speak to the class, and then the entire mass of thirdlings and humans continued around the perimeter until they were beside the restrained orcs.

The massive hominids were sitting on the floor with their backs to the wall, each of them chained by the neck and waist. They were surrounded by their own filth, and the smell was intense. Their heads hung down loosely as if they were asleep, but the nearest one looked up as the group approached. Desmond's gut wrenched when he saw the creature's face. There were scars upon scars, with some wounds so recent the dried blood hadn't worn off. Drool moistened the creature's chin and dripped onto its lap. It was a man, but the orc beside it was a woman, although one of her breasts had been mutilated so badly it was mostly gone. The third orc's body was too ravaged to even tell if it was male or female.

The huge man's dull eyes widened slightly when he spotted Desmond and the other humans, and he let out a grunt. The other two raised their heads to look. Both of them had the faces of beaten, pitiful creatures, devoid of any spirit they may have ever had. All three orcs grunted as they stared at the humans.

One of the fighting instructors stepped forward to talk to her class. She pointed at the humans and the restrained orcs as she spoke, and several times she swung her mace in the air as if reenacting the killing of the orc at the fence the previous day. When she finally fell silent, the mass of kids raised their quivering hands and shouted, "*Loo-roh-roh-roh.*"

"It seems your brave deed is becoming folktale fodder," Zachariah said.

"Which means they admire and respect us," Lorissa added. "This is a good thing."

The storytelling instructor approached the male orc and kicked its scarred and meaty foot. It shifted its gaze from the humans to her face but didn't move. She then pulled back and struck its foot viciously with her mace. The orc howled and drew up its knee, cupping its bleeding foot in one hand. The instructor raised the mace, threatening another strike, and the orc rolled to its side and got to its feet. It was broad and stood well over seven feet tall, but there wasn't an ounce of defiance or threat in its demeanor. It was now an empty shell, regardless of what it had once been.

The instructor spoke to the young thirdlings again as she purposely approached Infinity and handed her the mace. She then stepped back and motioned for Infinity to use the mace on the orc.

After gazing at the instructor for a moment, Infinity lowered the mace to her side and shook her head. "To hell with that."

9

———————

TRADING POST

August 26 - 9:24 AM

INFINITY WAS A FIGHTER. Always had been. And she was even a fighting instructor. But something about this situation triggered her seldom-used sense of mercy. These orcs were not a threat to anyone.

"You should do what they want," Lorissa said. "We need their help."

Infinity glared at the scientist. "You really want to tell me what to do?"

Lorissa lowered her eyes and shook her head.

The thirdling instructor gestured again, leaving no doubt about what she wanted Infinity to do.

"Perhaps you don't have to kill it," Zachariah said. "I believe they simply wish to learn from you."

Infinity turned to Desmond. He said, "If we end up bridging the colony here, don't we want the thirdlings to know who we really are? We're a compassionate species, right?"

Infinity had her doubts about the truth of that, but the fact of the matter was that she wasn't going to kill this helpless man. Perhaps he had once been a brutal killer himself, but she just wasn't going to do it. If the thirdlings wanted a fighting lesson, though, she could do that.

She handed the mace back to the instructor. The small woman gestured yet again for Infinity to use it instead. So Infinity dropped the mace at the woman's feet, turned to the orc, and closed the distance in three steps. She spun to her left and launched off on her right foot into a 540 roundhouse kick. Her bare foot connected loudly with the orc's forehead, a blow that would have put any human on the ground. She completed the turn and landed on her feet. The orc howled but barely staggered back, which was the result she had hoped for. The 540 kick wasn't really a hardcore fighting move, but it was showy and impressive. And she had used it effectively on nonhuman opponents that couldn't possibly have seen it coming.

Immediately the young thirdlings shook their raised hands. "*Loo-roh-roh-roh!*"

Infinity walked away from the orcs toward the center of the room. "Watch what I do," she said. She then went through the initial turn of the 540 kick in slow motion and pointed to her right leg. "Launch from the same foot you're kicking with."

She went through the entire kick at full speed and then repeated the slow motion approach. The two instructors caught on to what she was doing. They each tried the move themselves, and soon the entire class was jumping about, trying to replicate the kick. With their small bodies and thin legs, Infinity couldn't imagine they could do much damage with this move, but they seemed determined to learn it.

For the next half hour or so, Infinity was kept busy with thirty-inch-tall thirdlings wanting personal assistance. Occasionally she glanced at the three orcs. They had all returned to their original position with heads hanging over their laps, sleeping or staring at nothing.

If things had gone differently during the last twenty-four hours, she and the other humans would likely be dead or chained to that wall with the orcs.

1:09 PM

THE PRICE of armor was comfort and mobility, which was why Infinity had always preferred to fight wearing minimal clothing. But the thirdlings obviously believed heavily armored wagons were the only way to venture beyond the village's perimeter fence. It was hotter than hell in the boxy passenger cabin. Not only that, but the space had been designed for the thirdlings' smaller bodies.

She glanced at the thirdlings Desmond had named Jane, Bill, and Hickok. She then fiddled with the thick, copper window panel beside her until it popped open. She got to her knees on the seat and forced her head and shoulders through the opening for some fresh air. Following behind the wagon were three nearly-identical wagons, loaded with thirdlings and various goods. Each wagon was being pulled by two camels.

Beyond the other wagons, about a quarter mile back, the perimeter fence gate they'd passed through was still visible. Infinity gazed at the hills surrounding the thirdling village and felt a disorienting familiarity with the layout of the terrain. They were the same hills that surrounded SafeTrek on her own world. During the past four years, she had grown to think of those hills as her home. With a divergence point of only 210,000 years ago, there was no reason to be surprised that the hills looked the same on this world. But still it seemed strange to Infinity, as it had on other excursions before this one. At this moment, the wagon was rolling over the same ground where several hundred people had been killed in a storm two days ago on her world.

She turned and looked forward. In the distance was another tall fence. But this one surrounded only a small area, maybe an acre. Next to the fence were more armored wagons, with thirdlings moving about between them. She pulled herself back in. "Looks like we're about there."

"Although we have no idea where *there* is," Zachariah replied.

He was right. The thirdlings had insisted the humans come along on this excursion, but of course explanations weren't possible. Since they had brought four wagons, Infinity had assumed it was a trading mission. But for all she knew, they could be headed for a barbecue—with them as the main course.

They passed through a gate into the fenced enclosure, joining the other wagons that were now already inside. When the humans emerged into the sunlight, thirdlings—presumably from other villages, due to the different copper ornaments hanging from their necks—gathered around, chattering and pointing.

In the center of the fenced enclosure was a fortified, white-domed structure, similar to those back in the village. This was either a single-family dwelling, which was unlikely, or it was a safe meeting place for thirdlings from different villages. A neutral trading post, perhaps.

Several lyrical voices rose above the rest, and thirdlings pointed through the fence to the south. Infinity stepped closer and peered through the slats. A group of seven hominids were walking across the open field between hills. They were too far to see much detail, but their large size and slumped posture indicated they were orcs. They stopped and gazed toward the enclosure, but then they continued on their way. Either they didn't care to investigate, or they had already learned the cost of trying to climb the fence.

The thirdlings turned from the fence and continued their

conversation, apparently not concerned. The talking continued, and before long the other thirdlings came closer to the humans, even reaching up to touch their faces and bald scalps.

The female Desmond had named Jane brought out her wide book with blank pages, and then they all moved into the domed structure. Desmond sat on the floor with the thirdlings as they passed around the pictures he'd drawn. Infinity remained standing and watched carefully as they looked at the drawing that was supposed to inform them that many other humans would show up. They definitely were interested, but the only thirdling facial expression she thought she understood was their broad smile. And they were not smiling at this picture.

Actually, Infinity had already pretty much ruled out this world as a viable colony destination. The thirdlings and orcs presented too many problems, in spite of what Lorissa wanted to believe.

A male thirdling from the spiral ornament village approached Infinity and stared up at her. He then reached up and poked her right breast several times with his finger, like he was trying to prove to himself it was real. She gritted her teeth and resisted the urge to push him away. He smiled at her, for whatever that was worth. He then held up his other hand. In it was a pile of small copper rings. He picked up one of the rings and held it up, revealing that they were actually joined together. It was two short chains with horseshoe-shaped fittings at each end. And there was a circular ring around the chain links between the two ends.

The little man said something to Infinity and then turned his back to her. A few seconds later, he turned back around, holding the circular ring separate from the chain. He turned his back to her again, and when he turned around the ring was back on the chain between the horseshoes.

He handed her the chain.

"It's a puzzle," Zachariah said. "I think I can—"

"Yeah, I got that. He wants to see how smart we are. I've been through this crap before."

Zachariah became antsy, pointing at the puzzle and barely stopping himself from snatching it from her. "If you just... you have to turn them. And then...."

She thrust the rings into his eager hands.

He arranged the circular ring at an angle to the two ends, folded the horseshoes over on top of each other, and slipped the ring off.

"*Loo-roh-roh-roh!*" the thirdling sang.

"Give me that." Infinity snatched the puzzle pieces from Zachariah. She tried putting them back together, but she hadn't watched his motions carefully enough.

The door flew open and a thirdling armed with a bow rushed in. "*Jila-lor-lor-lor! Jiheela-lor-lor-lor!*"

All the thirdlings stopped what they were doing and gathered at the window slits. Before Infinity got to one of the slits, she heard a commotion outside—the musical babbling of thirdlings intermingling with orc grunts. She leaned over the heads of several thirdlings to look out. Thirdlings stood facing the fence, ready to shoot arrows at several orcs peering in at them. She counted five orcs, but she could tell by the thirdlings' pointing and glancing over their shoulders that there must have been more beyond the range of her vision. Compared to the orcs she'd seen at the fence the previous day, these seemed only curious. And the thirdlings' casual chattering meant they weren't all that concerned.

One of the thirdlings pulled on her hand. It was the female, Jane, trying to pull her toward the door.

Infinity resisted. "What?"

Jane held out a bladed mace and gestured for Infinity to take it outside.

"Screw you. You can fight your own battles." Infinity then realized most of the other thirdlings were watching her, many of them smiling and shaking their flattened hands. She should not have insisted yesterday on fighting that damn orc.

Desmond stepped to her side. "I think we should stay inside. Remember how the orcs reacted—"

"I know! I don't intend to go out there."

But the thirdlings were becoming more insistent. Some of them had resorted to gleeful chanting.

"We need them as allies," Lorissa said. "Why are you ignoring them?"

Infinity thought briefly of putting the mace into Lorissa's hands and shoving her out the door. But bridgers didn't harm tourists. She turned and squinted through the window slit again. The orcs were pacing back and forth outside the fence, occasionally shoving their fingers through the gaps and gripping the slats like they were testing for weaknesses. What would they do to these thirdlings if the fence wasn't there? Obviously the thirdlings were capable of capturing and imprisoning the larger species, but most likely those were individuals that had been shot and injured—perhaps while at the fence like these were—and left behind by the other orcs.

The thirdlings surrounded Infinity, pushing and pulling her toward the door. The damn things were relentless. She now had two choices: violently resist or go along. As much as Infinity distrusted Lorissa, the scientist was right. This wasn't the time to antagonize the thirdlings. So she allowed them to pull her through the door.

She straightened up and shielded her eyes from the sun. Jane took Infinity's other hand and pressed the mace handle into her palm until she accepted it. The orcs were still pacing back and forth by the fence, and it was now definite that there were more of them, maybe as many as twenty.

Jane gestured toward the fence, so Infinity stepped closer. She stopped only a few feet from the nearest orc. The creature seemed to notice her and stopped pacing. It pressed its face to the fence, gazing down at her through a three-inch gap in the slats. Its fingers came through a gap at the level of Infinity's eyes and gripped the fence, knuckles white in spite of a lifetime of scars and filth. The massive creature sniffed the air. It then let out a sharp snort, "*Chuh!*"

Infinity looked up into its eyes and spoke gently. "I'm not a threat to you. You have no reason to hate me."

The creature's eyes narrowed. "*Chuh. Chuh. Chuh! Chuh!*" It slammed its forehead into the fence and yanked on the slat. The dry piece of wood cracked, and the orc ripped it away. The creature hunched over and glared at Infinity through a new ten-inch gap. "*Chuh! Chuh!*"

Several other orcs were now at its side, and when they saw Infinity, they began grunting and howling. An arm the size of Infinity's leg shot through the widened gap, and she stepped back to avoid being grabbed.

A thirdling stepped up beside Infinity and pulled back her short bow. She waited for an orc to put its face to the gap and then released. With a sharp *thunk*, the arrow penetrated the creature's left eye socket. Without even convulsing, the creature fell to the ground, dead.

The orcs—all twenty of them—became silent, staring at their fallen companion.

"*Chuh. Chuh. Chuh! Chuh!*" The grunting grew and intensified and then gave way to feral shrieks of rage. The orcs threw themselves against the fence, pounding and screaming. Several began climbing, although they would have to negotiate the downward-pointing spikes at the top. Three of the orcs began a cooperative effort to widen the gap by pulling free another slat. The board cracked, and seconds later an orc shoved its entire head through a gap that was now at least sixteen inches wide.

It was too late to stop the conflict now, so Infinity stepped forward and struck the orc's forehead with her mace. The creature howled and drew back. But numerous hands appeared on the next board and the orcs began pulling. If they removed one more slat, the gap might be big enough for them to squeeze through it.

Infinity hammered the orcs' fingers, slicing them mercilessly. "Help me!" she cried over her shoulder. One of the thirdlings with an axe rushed to her side and together they chopped at the hands.

But there were too many of them. And the orcs were watching through the gaps, pulling their fingers back just before being hit. Just as another thirdling with a mace joined in the effort, the third board began to crack.

A hand gripped Infinity's shoulder. "They're coming over the fence," Desmond said. "We need to get inside."

Infinity glanced up. Two orcs, bloodied from the spikes and with thirdling arrows protruding from their bodies, were swinging their legs over the top of the fence. Several more were still negotiating the spikes.

The third slat gave way with a loud crack. Immediately, an orc rammed its way headfirst through the opening, stopped only by its thick chest. The thirdling next to Infinity swung at its face with her axe. In a blur of motion, the orc grabbed her arm with one hand, pulled her closer, and then seized her neck with its other hand. Within a split second, the thirdling's face was in the orc's mouth. The orc bit down, crushing the tiny face and tearing the thirdling's skin from her skull. The orc released the writhing body and furiously struggled to push through the opening. Several arrows hit its face but were deflected by its dense skull.

"Let's go, Infinity!"

She turned away from the fence. "Where are the tourists?"

"Still inside. Come on!"

She gave in and followed him. The thirdlings had come to the same conclusion and were crowding against the door, pushing through one at a time.

A loud *thud* pulled Infinity's attention back to the fence. An orc had fallen to the ground inside the enclosure. But it was incapacitated by at least a dozen arrows and couldn't get up.

Another orc landed on its feet beside the first. Several thirdlings rushed forward, forming a half circle around it, and shot arrows into its neck and chest from five feet away. The orc lunged forward, grabbed one of the thirdlings, and swung the smaller creature over its head, intending to club the others with it. But then it paused, coughing up blood. Its chest heaved as it tried to suck in air. In one last defiant move, it hurled the thirdling at the others, hitting two of them. It then collapsed to the ground, blood gushing from its nose and mouth.

Another board cracked as the orc in the fence pushed through. Grunting and screaming, it fought its way through the opening.

"Infinity!"

She turned. Desmond was halfway through the small door, holding a hand out to her.

"Go on," she cried. He ducked through and she followed.

Seconds later, the last of the surviving thirdlings entered the structure and latched the door securely from the inside.

Almost immediately, orcs began pounding on the door. But it had been built to sustain such an attack, and soon the pounding relented. Thirdlings stood by the window slits with bows ready, but the orcs were apparently smart enough to keep their distance.

Infinity moved to a window slit that allowed her to see some of the wagons parked outside. As she suspected, the orcs had given up trying to break into the domed fortress and were now focusing their attention on the camels. She had yet to see the huge men using weapons of any kind, but two of them approached one of the camels with broken fence slats. They raised the slats over their heads and began pounding the beast, the boards clattering against the camel's copper armor. Several orcs grabbed the camel's feet and pulled. The camel grunted and fell to its side. The orcs leapt on it, tearing away the armor plates and pummeling the creature with their fists. One of them attacked the creature's neck with its teeth.

Gradually the camel quit kicking and lay still. The orcs began feeding, tearing off long strips of hide with their teeth and then biting off chunks of red muscle tissue.

"*Loo-roh-roh-roh! Loo-roh-roh-roh!*"

Infinity turned away from the window. The thirdlings were actually smiling at each other as they chanted, in spite of the fact that several of their companions lay dead outside.

She plopped her butt on the floor and leaned against the wall. Desmond came over and sat beside her, which prompted Zachariah and Lorissa to do the same, although Lorissa was careful to sit where the two men were between her and Infinity.

"I've heard stories about neverlands," Infinity said. "Alternate worlds you'd actually *want* to go to. But I've sure as hell never seen one. This world's as screwed up as any of them."

"At least we're safe in here," Desmond said. "I'd guess four more hours until bridge-back."

"Which brings us to an inevitable dilemma," Zachariah said. "Reece Eagleton has made it abundantly and painfully clear that we will have only sixty minutes after bridge-back to make a determination of this world's viability. What do we tell him?"

"What do you think?" Infinity asked him.

Zachariah shook his head. "It's problematic, to say the least."

She turned to Lorissa with raised brows.

The agriculture scientist looked down at the floor. "You know how I feel about it."

"I don't see what there is to discuss," Desmond said. "If your colony were twenty or thirty people, I imagine these thirdlings would take you in. Or at least help you get established. But over 700 people?" He shook his head.

"I agree," Infinity said. "So three out of four of us give it a thumbs down. Lorissa, when we bridge back, I'm sure you'll have a chance to express your opinion, but for the sake of your colony, I recommend you keep it to yourself. You need to trust me when I say this world is screwed up."

"But you said they're *all* screwed up."

Infinity stared at her, but Lorissa simply looked back down at the floor.

"You've got to be kidding," Zachariah said. "Why are they in such a festive mood?" He was watching the center of the room, where about twenty thirdlings were engaged in some kind of dance, similar to the one they'd shown the humans yesterday back in the village.

As Infinity watched, she began suspecting the activity was more than just a dance. It was now obvious the thirdlings were clustered together in village-based groups, about seven per group. There were thirdlings from three villages, represented by copper ornaments: fish, spirals, and a third design that was some kind of four-legged animal with no tail.

With the three groups arranged in a rough circle facing the center, the thirdlings slapped their hands against their thighs, creating a simple, primitive rhythm. Each individual danced in place, apparently using random freestyle moves. But each group also moved as a unit. The three village groups drifted toward the center and then passed through each other until they ended up on opposite sides. As they passed each other, still dancing, some of them would throw one leg out toward another. At first Infinity thought they were trying to trip each other, because the others would quickly attempt to avoid contact with the thrown legs. But on several occasions, thirdlings watching from the sidelines cheered and pointed, obviously impressed by a successful move, although no thirdlings were tripped.

Eventually it became clear that a successful move involved one thirdling placing a foot between the feet of another thirdling in a certain way. And every time the three groups would converge and pass through each other, several thirdlings would execute a successful move, to the delight of their fellow villagers, and several would fail, to the delight of their opponents.

Jane stepped in front of the humans and held out copper cups of the dark alcoholic ale. Infinity refused, but the other three accepted their cups. Infinity then realized most of the other thirdlings already had their own cups. Some of them even had two.

While orcs slaughtered and ate their camels outside, these thirdlings were having a goddamn dance party.

10

───────

FIGHTING

August 26 - 5:37 PM

THE DANCING GAME was harder than it looked. Desmond had tried for the last three rounds, much to the delight of the thirdlings, but he had yet to score a point for his village—assuming points were even used. Of course it would have helped had he understood exactly where to place his foot to score a point. And it might have helped if he'd turned down that second cup of stout.

The orcs had finally wandered off, leaving behind an undetermined number of dead camels. But still the festive gathering had gone on, as if it were more important than the livestock or the thirdlings that had been killed in the attack. About an hour ago, some of the thirdlings had taken one of the wagons and exited the enclosure, but that hadn't stalled the festivities.

When the current round of dancing ended, Desmond stepped away before the thirdlings could convince him to try again. Exhausted, he sat down beside Infinity and the two scientists. "If things weren't going to hell back home, it'd be easier to appreciate that we're the only humans who will ever meet these amazing creatures."

Infinity eyed him for a moment. "Somehow it doesn't surprise me you'd say that."

"Am I too wide-eyed and green for your taste?"

She didn't smile, but the muscles in her face relaxed a little. "Maybe it provides balance. Armando said I'm wound pretty goddamn tight."

Desmond feigned like he was starting to get up. "Would you care to dance, then?"

"Don't push it," she said.

Zachariah cleared his throat. "Well, this explains a few things."

Desmond gave him a bridger's scowl and saw from the corner of his eye that Infinity was doing the same. Zachariah just grinned.

A commotion outside drew Desmond to his feet, and he looked out. The wagon that had departed an hour ago was returning, and now it was clear why it had left in the first place. Tied to it were four extra camels, complete with copper armor, no doubt to replace those the orcs had killed.

The thirdlings heard the noise as well and finally the dancing competition came to a stop. The party was over.

Once outside, the thirdlings gathered at the wagons, where they spent the next half hour inspecting each other's goods and making trades. There were rolls of brightly-colored fabric, as well as completed pairs of shorts, apparently the only item of clothing the thirdlings wore this time of the year. There were long, warm-looking robes, perhaps the standard clothing they'd all be wearing in the coming colder months. There were axes, maces, bows, and arrows. Numerous copper canisters were opened and passed around, their contents smelled by all before decisions were made regarding their worth. Bundles of dried meat, tied together with string, were sampled and traded, although there were no signs of bread or any other plant-based foods. And most of all, there was copper: copper arm and leg bands, copper ornaments, copper plates and cups, and numerous items with purposes Desmond could only guess.

A multi-village team of thirdlings unloaded some long boards and set about repairing the damaged fence. The orcs had killed four of the more than twenty camels, although they had eaten portions of only two. These carcasses were stripped of their armor, dragged out using the living camels, and left to rot in the grass about fifty yards from the gate. The thirdlings then hitched the replacement camels to the wagons.

Three dead thirdlings were loaded into one of the wagons. Desmond noticed the orc carcasses were gone, presumably dragged away by their companions.

While all of this was happening, several thirdlings kept a vigilant watch over the surrounding area, making it obvious why they had constructed this fortified trading post in the middle of a relatively flat and treeless valley between forested hills.

At one point, there was a brief pause when the lookouts spotted orcs at about three hundred yards out. Standing near the edge of the trees, the creatures—perhaps eight of them—watched the enclosure. But the next time Desmond looked their way, they were gone.

By the time the trading and maintenance chores were complete, the sun had dropped low in the western sky. It was probably at least 6:00 PM, and bridge-back was at seven.

The thirdlings went through a ritual that was obviously their way of saying goodbye. One at a time, they approached each other. Each of them raised one hand, and they pressed their palms together at the height of their faces. Musical words were spoken during each of these encounters, but it seemed to Desmond that the words were different each time. A few thirdlings from the two other villages even tried this with the humans and smiled at the attempts to match the gesture.

Jane, Bill, and Hickok became relatively quiet on the ride back to the village. The three gazed at the humans, who were uncomfortably crammed into thirdling-sized seats, and soon their disproportionately large eyes became glazed over and half-shut. Not surprising, considering they each probably weighed under sixty pounds and had imbibed several cups of stout.

Desmond wondered what the thirdlings would think when he and the other humans vanished into thin air at 7:00 PM, which as far as he knew could be at any moment. He found it odd that he was concerned about frightening these creatures. Yes, they had been friendly. But they were also quite capable of staggering cruelty, as shown by the captive orcs they kept alive for fighting practice.

No doubt there had been a long, complicated history of interaction between these two hominid species. And perhaps even a third species, if Jane's drawings were accurate. As an outsider, it was too easy to assume this extreme level of fear and violence could have been avoided. Desmond had to remind himself that similar conflicts and cruelties had frequently occurred on his own world. And that was between races that were only moderately different from each other, within a single species. He could scarcely imagine how much worse the cruelties would be if more than one hominid species had continued to coexist on his world.

His thoughts turned to the Outlanders, the alien civilization that had intentionally destroyed other civilized worlds by sending plans for the bridging device. Desmond's own world had now become a victim of the Outlanders' trickery. The physics of information transmission dictated that the Outlanders could not have known which civilizations they were destroying. But what if they somehow *did* know? Perhaps they somehow knew the cruelties humans were capable of and had selectively targeted Earth—as a kindness to other civilizations living in the same corner of the galaxy.

Desmond blinked and shook his head, trying to clear this stomach-churning thought. But it persisted. He turned to Infinity. "Do you think we deserve what's happening to our world? Humans, I mean."

She studied him for a moment. "That's what you're worried about?"

"Don't you think about it sometimes?"

"No."

"Why not?"

She sighed. "I've been a fighter all my life, even before I did it for money. Fighting is fast. It's quick. No time for thinking, just for instinct and muscle memory from training. You don't get to decide who's right and who's wrong. No time for that. And it wouldn't matter anyway, because that's all made-up shit."

Desmond frowned at her. "You think what's right and wrong is just made up?"

"Isn't it?"

"I suppose on some level, but—"

"On *every* level. Think of the bridger's creed. It's supposed to represent right and wrong for our profession. But now even that's changing. You think you know what's right, and then someone decides it's not. You think you know what's wrong, and then someone does something that proves they have a different concept of what's wrong. It's all made up." She shifted in her tiny seat and leaned closer, her eyes intense. "Anyone can take anything from you, Desmond. Except for one thing they can't take—your will to fight. So you fight to keep what you want to keep, whether it's your stuff or your life."

Again, Desmond realized how Infinity's world view had been shaped by a life very different from his own.

She went on. "You're wasting your time wondering why the Outlanders destroy other civilizations. Everyone has a different right and wrong, including the Outlanders. So don't worry about it. Now we only have time to fight."

Desmond glanced at Lorissa and Zachariah. Both scientists were listening but apparently content to do so silently. He then turned to the thirdlings. All three of them now had their eyes closed, their heads bobbing like tired children on the ride home from a long day at the beach.

And then the thirdlings, as well as the entire wagon, were gone.

11

MINUTES

August 26 - 7:00 PM

INFINITY HAD no time to straighten her body, so she hit the padded floor of the bridging chamber still in a sitting position.

Zachariah was the first to speak. "Ow! That was unexpected. Great, I'm naked again." He then doubled over and retched.

Beside him, Lorissa was already dry heaving.

Infinity did a quick visual survey of her three companions sprawled on the floor around her. "We're all okay," she shouted. "No serious injuries."

Armando's voice came over the comm. "Welcome back! Glad to see you're all safe."

The airlock hatch opened and med techs in white biosuits rushed in. They went straight to the two scientists and helped them to their feet. Zachariah and Lorissa told them they could walk, so the techs led them out the airlock and to the med lab.

"I assume, then, that the world is viable?" Armando asked.

Infinity shook her head as she got to her feet. "No, it's not."

This was followed by a few seconds of silence.

"But you're all alive and appear to be healthy." It was Reece Eagleton.

Desmond stood up beside Infinity. "It's not that simple."

"It couldn't be any simpler," Eagleton said. "You're alive and—"

Armando cut him off. "This can wait. Let's give them five minutes to get their bearings and hydrate a bit. Infinity and Desmond, we'll see you in the post-bridging interview chamber."

There was a click as Armando switched off the comm, and Infinity saw the two men exchanging words behind the plexiglass barrier.

Desmond was holding his gut. "Jesus, does this ever get easier?"

"That Eagleton's an asshole," Infinity said. "Come on, let's get some water."

He nodded. And then he frowned. "Why do I still feel the alcohol?"

"It's in your cells, so it bridged back with you. Why do people who drink always complain about the effects?"

He huffed out an abrupt laugh. "I deserved that."

Exactly five minutes later, Infinity, Desmond, Zachariah, and Lorissa filed into the interview room and sat behind the waist-high barrier. Instead of being naked, they each wore a paper gown— another long-standing policy that no longer mattered.

Armando and Eagleton sat waiting for them on the other side of the plexiglass. Just the two, which was a little surprising. Infinity had assumed, with the fate of 718 refugees on the line, a few more people might participate in this decision. At least some of the refugees themselves.

"What's happened since our departure?" Lorissa asked.

"Nothing good," Eagleton replied with a frown. "Another massive wind storm in the region, north of Little Rock. Could be five hundred dead. More earthquakes worldwide. No way to even estimate the deaths from those yet. And no way to estimate deaths from suicide and homicide. Hell in a handbasket, as they say. Which is why we need to get these colonies off this planet."

"About that," Zachariah said. "The world we just assessed is not viable for our colony."

"Why not?"

"We'll explain," Zachariah replied, "but we think you should begin preparing another bio-probe rather than preparing the refugees."

"We don't all think that," Lorissa said.

Infinity wanted to grab the woman by the throat. She had warned her to keep her mouth shut.

Lorissa went on. "There is another species of hominid there. We call them thirdlings, and they were kind enough to—"

Eagleton held up a hand. "You know what? I'm going to stop you right there, because there simply isn't time. You people have returned alive, which is all we really need to know. This simple criterion is a new directive straight from President Millwright. And so we are not initiating another bio-probe. Your people have been segmented into groups and are prepared to bridge, one group per hour for the next thirty-six hours."

The two rooms fell silent. Infinity had expected an argument, but nothing like this. She rose to her feet, trying to stay calm. "The world isn't viable for more than a few dozen people. Maybe fifty."

Armando held both hands up to intervene. "Listen to what she's saying, Reece. She's not one to exaggerate."

Eagleton's eyes narrowed. "Doyle, you were there when I got the order from President Millwright. You were standing right next to me! Did it sound to you like there was room for negotiation?"

Armando turned back to the plexiglass. "It *was* the order, Infinity. Worsening conditions are heightening the urgency. We're having additional generators and personnel brought to SafeTrek, but this building itself could be destroyed at any time. The bridging facility in Dubai has already been lost. And we're waiting to hear if the Chinese facility has survived their most recent quake."

"Worldwide, we've bridged only six colonies from Earth," Eagleton added. "Six. That's 4,300 people. Out of eight billion."

Infinity closed her eyes for a moment, not only to control her anger, but to contemplate the reality of what she'd just been told.

"You people have returned alive," Eagleton repeated. "That means your colony will have a much better chance there than they would here. I think you know what their chances are here. I certainly know, because unlike you, I do not have a place in a refugee group. Nor does my family."

Infinity stared at him. The guy was an asshole, but he was afraid. And the fact that he was here now, doing this instead of spending his final days with his family, was something.

"Do you even want to hear our report?" Infinity asked.

Eagleton nodded. "If you insist. But your time may be better spent preparing." He looked at his watch. "You'll be escorting the first group in less than forty-five minutes. If you refuse, they'll go without your help." He turned to Zachariah and Lorissa. "If you or those in your colony refuse, we have a second colony right behind them who are terrified their turn is going to be too late. I'm sure they'll jump at the chance to move forward."

"I can't believe this is happening," Desmond muttered.

"We can make it work," Lorissa said. "Infinity, with your help we can do this! There's already a strong perimeter fence, and good dwellings. And livestock, and weapons. We can spread out into two villages if we have to. Or even three."

"And the thirdlings?" Desmond asked.

Lorissa pursed her lips and shook her head slightly. "I don't have all the answers."

Infinity was thinking seriously of blurting out the agriculture scientist's dark secret. She looked the woman in the eye. "Do you want to bridge with your colony?"

Lorissa's eyes widened. "Yes."

"Then stop talking. Now."

7:33 *PM*

THE PICNIC TABLE was still missing from the training field behind SafeTrek. Where could it have blown to? Of course, it wasn't really important, but at this moment it annoyed Infinity that no one had bothered to find it and put it back where it belonged. And the grass needed mowing, too. Just one thing. It would be nice if just one damn thing were the same as before.

The very fact that she was out here a half hour after bridging back was unprecedented. Normally, she'd endure three days of chemo-cleansing and patho-cleansing before getting the chance to put on clothes and leave the lab. But even that didn't matter anymore, as long as she stayed clear of the members of the next colony in line behind Lorissa's.

She ripped off her paper gown and sat naked in the grass. The surrounding forest had been chewed up by the storm, changing the scenery to an alien landscape. Another goddamn thing that had changed.

Desmond came through the metal door at the rear of the building and walked out to join her. He seemed to waver for a moment and then took off his own paper gown and sat beside her. He took a long drink from his bottle of protein water. "I'm already exhausted. How're we supposed to help refugees for the next thirty-six hours?"

She shrugged. She didn't feel the need to talk. It was just good having him there. "Maybe we'll die."

"Optimistic as ever," he said.

She shrugged again.

"I was going to eat," he said, "but it's too close to bridging for that." He ran his hands through the grass like he was grooming it. "Do you think there's any chance they'll survive? The colonists?"

"Maybe. I hate myself for saying it, but their best bet might be if they make Lorissa their leader. But I'm glad we're not going to be there long enough to see that happen."

"Jesus, you have an interesting mind. I wouldn't have even thought of that. Actually, it makes me want to throw up."

She shrugged again. "I almost stopped her."

"Lorissa? How?"

"I know something. She'd be thrown out of the colony if Eagleton knew."

He thumped her elbow with two knuckles. "She told you something last night, didn't she? When she ran from the thirdling house? I knew something was up."

"She killed her own father."

"What? Lorissa did?"

Infinity glanced at him. "It's kind of a long story, and the minutes are passing fast."

He nodded.

"I want to sit with you," she said.

He understood, and he unfolded his legs. She moved over between them and leaned her bald head back on the smooth skin of his chest.

Cicadas were starting to sing in the broken forest, but even those were fewer, quieter. Most of them had been crushed in the storm.

7:52 PM - Group 1

. . .

Twenty people stood in the bridging chamber, most of them too terrified to talk. The room smelled of sweat and urine. At least one of them had peed right there on the floor. That's how scared they were. And there wasn't much Infinity could think of to say that would be comforting.

Two bridgers, the two scientists, and sixteen refugees. Infinity had never bridged with a group larger than three tourists.

She and Desmond had already taken their technetium-99m, both orally and by injection. This radioisotope would decay in their bodies until just over 1.5% remained, and then the bridging device would pull them back. The scientists and the sixteen refugees had not been dosed with technetium. For them this was a one-way bridge.

They had every right to be terrified.

Only a few minutes left, and this was Infinity's first opportunity to talk to these refugees since returning from the recent excursion. What could she possibly say?

She had to at least try. "Listen up! I want to see everyone's eyes!" She waited. "Bridging doesn't hurt, but it will make you want to vomit. If so, just go with it. Not much will come out anyway. You're going to drop a foot or so to the ground, but not enough to hurt you. Just be ready to balance yourself. I want you to stand like this." She demonstrated, and as far as she could tell, they all spread their legs apart and bent their knees. "Some of you decided to keep your clothes on until bridging. I don't care about that, as long as you understand that your clothing and your hair will be gone when you hit the ground on your new world. Don't freak out about it."

She took a moment to scan their faces. The rest of the world envied these people for having a spot in this colony, but at this moment, Infinity pitied every one of them.

"Now, this is new and important information. Knowing it may save your lives." She turned to look at the plexiglass window.

"Armando, you need to either record this or repeat it yourself for every one of the groups following us. Okay?"

Celia was standing next to Armando, and she looked down and touched a control. "You got it, Infinity. I'm recording."

Infinity turned back to the refugees. "You're going to drop into a fenced-in pasture. Unless they've been removed, there will be a herd of camels in the pasture. They're harmless. There will be a tall perimeter fence about a hundred yards away. Don't go near that fence. It's there to keep out a dangerous human-like creature. They're huge, strong, and mean as hell. The fence was constructed by a much smaller human-like creature we call thirdlings. So far they seem friendly. And to be honest, you have little chance of surviving without them. Don't threaten them. Don't startle them. Smile at them whenever you can."

She glanced over at Lorissa before going on. "I can't lie to you people—it's going to be a challenge to mesh over 700 humans into the culture of these thirdlings." She shook her head. "You may have to be separated into very small groups to make it work."

This resulted in a few gasps and at least one shocked sob. Wisely, Lorissa had remained silent through all this.

Infinity went on. "I'm not sure how to say this, but I have to try. You may reach a point where you feel your efforts are failing. You may believe your only chance of survival is to become something worse than the creatures beyond that tall perimeter fence." Again she glanced at Lorissa.

"If you do reach that point, no one can blame you. I've been at that point myself, more than once. When we're faced with annihilation, we have to fight. But listen to me, please. It is the *point* at which we decide we must become monsters. It is that point—that threshold—that is important. If you want to be a colony worthy of this chance you've been given, then that threshold is everything. Please don't hit that threshold until your annihilation is certain. Not before then. Try everything you can—every possible strategy—

to live peacefully with the thirdlings. Finally, if nothing works, if your destruction is certain, then become the monster you never wanted to be. Fight. Scratch and bite and kill."

She looked around at their faces. They were more terrified now than before. Good. They needed to be.

"I don't want to do this," a man in his forties said. He walked toward the closed hatch. "I want out."

"I want out, too," a woman said, sobbing. "I just want to go home."

A waft of fresh urine moved across the chamber.

"One minute, Infinity," Celia said.

Infinity gently took the man's arm and guided him away from the hatch. "It's too late, sir. Stand with your legs apart. That's good. Now relax."

Armando's voice came through the comm. "Godspeed to you all. Infinity, I'm proud of you, kiddo. Desmond, take care of her. She's not as tough as she wants you to think she is."

Infinity raised her middle finger toward the plexiglass just before the room vanished.

12

———————————

INVENTORY

August 26 - 8:oo PM

Desmond's ears were assaulted by screams, grunts, and twenty naked bodies hitting the ground and jostling for room and balance. They all landed on their feet, but almost immediately they staggered and doubled over to retch. They were too close together for this, and the entire group began toppling over in a domino effect. The grunting and screaming crescendoed as the mass of confused refugees collapsed into a heap.

"Stop moving!" Infinity shouted.

The crowd quieted down only slightly, but the frantic motion stopped.

"Now get to your feet and help the person beside you."

Within a minute the worst of the retching had stopped and everyone was more-or-less upright.

Desmond looked around the area. The herd of camels stood a few hundred yards away, and some of them held their heads upright, staring over at the commotion. But no thirdlings were visible anywhere. The sun was just setting, and the area would be completely dark by the time the second group arrived. It looked like it would be a cloudless night with a quarter moon that was already fairly bright. The light would be helpful.

The group started spreading out, but Desmond said, "Wait! Stay where you are. Now, move out into a circle that encloses the area where all of you bridged in. Stand shoulder to shoulder." This took some time, because those that weren't still nauseous were busy feeling their bald scalps or gawking around at the scenery.

"The camels, there they are!" a woman said, pointing. The others looked, like tourists on a safari vacation. The camels were now running over to investigate.

The humans got into a circle just as the camels spread out and surrounded them, smacking their lips and apparently looking for handouts. Or maybe they were simply curious. Desmond told the refugees to ignore the creatures and pull up the grass at their feet by the roots, which would create a marked boundary around the bridge-in area.

Infinity nodded at him, realizing what he was having them do. "You need to stay out of this circle and keep everyone else out for the next thirty-five hours," she added.

Zachariah and Lorissa came over and stood beside the two bridgers as they watched the refugees pulling up grass. The camels were already feeding on the pulled grass that was being tossed aside.

Zachariah rubbed his chin. "Okay, well, what do we do now?"

Desmond looked at Infinity.

She exhaled loudly. "I've never done anything like this. I guess we need to take inventory." Louder, she said. "Listen up. How many of you have training or experience in combat or wilderness survival?"

Five hands went up, all of them men.

A stocky guy, possibly military, spoke up. "Ma'am, each colony has been assigned no fewer than 180 personnel with moderate to high skills. We were split up five per bridging team."

Desmond already knew this, and he was pretty sure Infinity did, too, but she didn't bother to say so. "I need you five over here."

The five men came over and stood beside her. All of them appeared to be in decent physical shape. The remaining eleven ranged from gaunt to moderately heavy. No one was over 250 pounds, under fifteen years old, or over sixty. Desmond didn't even want to contemplate the social injustices that must have occurred in selecting colony members. At least this group was somewhat racially diverse.

She spoke to the entire group. "I know all of you have other qualifications, and I hope you'll get to put them to use. But right now, the only thing that matters is survival." She pointed to the perimeter fence, although it was now almost obscured by darkness. "The giants—we call them orcs—are on the other side of that fence. The orcs will kill you on sight." She then pointed to the white domes of the village. "The thirdlings are there. The thirdlings are definitely our best bet."

She paused, and for a moment it looked like she wasn't sure what to say next. "You may think Desmond and I are here to protect you, because that's what bridgers used to do. But not any more. Everything has changed. If we have to fight to survive, we all fight. Every one of you. I won't be asking for volunteers."

"We don't have anything to fight with," a woman in her twenties said.

"We hope to get weapons from the thirdlings. But even so, don't underestimate what you can do with your bare hands."

The refugees glanced at each other in the fading light, obviously not convinced of this.

"We'd like to know what the plan is," said the man who had spoken first. "I was under the impression we'd be fashioning shelters, seeking out a source of water, making weapons, that sort of thing."

Infinity shook her head. "Things have changed. It's too dangerous to go beyond the perimeter fence, and here within the fence, our best bet is diplomacy with the thirdlings. Somehow we have to convince them to take all of you in, perhaps divide you into groups of only twenty or so per thirdling village."

"That's not the kind of colony we had in mind," a thin, black woman said.

"And it's not the only way!" It was Lorissa.

Infinity glared at her. "You need to think carefully about what you're doing, tourist."

Lorissa moved away from Infinity but obviously wasn't deterred. "This village has about 150 thirdlings, but they have at least forty well-built and sturdy shelters, most of them large enough to accommodate at least twenty of us. And they have land—plenty of land—already protected by perimeter fences. They have enough livestock to sustain our entire colony through the first winter."

Infinity stepped forward. Desmond's first thought was to grab her arm, but then it was too late. She closed the distance to Lorissa at a run. Before Lorissa could do anything more than widen her eyes, Infinity swung her right arm up, striking the woman's chin with the butt of her palm. The impact produced a sickening crunch, and Lorissa dropped to the ground, moaning and holding her jaw.

Infinity leaned over her. "You're going to stay down until I finish talking." She then turned to face the shocked refugees. "Lorissa's jaw is now broken. For those of you who don't really understand, in your new reality that means she's probably going to die."

Lorissa cried in pain, rolling back and forth on the ground.

"You're a bridger!" a woman shouted. "How could you do that?"

Desmond wondered how Infinity would answer that question, or if she even would.

"Shut up and listen!" she said. "You're the first group to bridge through. And from what I could see, you were about to make a suicidal decision based on Lorissa's influence—a decision you would have then pushed onto each of the groups arriving after you. Your entire colony would be at risk because of her stupidity." She pointed down at the still moaning woman. "Lorissa's not a bad person. And she may even be right. But she's got things turned around. You have to make peace with these thirdlings. It's your best chance. If it doesn't work, try again. And again. Only then, after every attempt fails, should you even consider the probably suicidal move of taking over their village. Even then, I doubt it would work, because other villages will likely come to their defense. Once you try that, you've permanently closed the door to peace."

She stepped closer to Lorissa and looked down at her. "With a broken jaw, you're going to die without the thirdlings' help. Maybe now you'll see the value of making peace with them."

9:01 PM - Group 2

JUST WHEN DESMOND was starting to wonder if something had gone wrong back home, the second group appeared and dropped to the ground within the marked bridge-in zone. In the last hour, his eyes had adjusted to the increasing darkness, but these new refugees were coming from a fully lit, white room. Completely blind, their bridge-in was even more chaotic than the first group's. They fell to the ground and floundered, a mass of thrashing arms and legs.

"You're okay!" Desmond shouted from the sideline. "Focus on my voice. Can everyone hear me?"

Amidst the cursing and retching, there were a few acknowledgements from those who were relatively calm. Desmond then put his hand on Zachariah's shoulder. "They're all yours, man." He then stepped back to let the parasitologist take over. This had been Infinity's idea. She'd pointed out the logic of having one of the colonists develop a pattern of leadership as soon as possible, and Zachariah was the logical choice. This would reduce the chance of a chaotic scramble for power after Desmond and Infinity bridged back.

The camel herd had eventually wandered off and disappeared into the darkness somewhere. The refugees from group one had fallen into somber silence, reluctant to interact with Infinity, although it had helped when she had ordered some of them to sit with Lorissa to comfort her. The tough-looking military guy, who had said his name was Leon, had stepped up and explained to the group that Infinity's logic was sound, regardless of her blunt-force tact. It would be suicide to try to take the thirdling's village. Desmond could see that Leon was likely to be a positive force in the colony's critical first days here. Hopefully, many more like him would bridge in with the remaining thirty-four groups.

Desmond sat on the ground next to Infinity and Leon. For some minutes, they watched Zachariah's orientation session with the new arrivals.

Finally, Leon said, "By my reckoning, when daylight arrives, we're going to have 240 folks sitting here in the grass, nude and vulnerable. By sunset tomorrow, we'll have five hundred. They're going to need water, and soon they'll need food. I figure there's a water source here for the livestock. How about you put a few of us to work finding it?"

Desmond nodded at the logic of this.

"No," Infinity said. Then she seemed to hesitate. "Well, I'll explain, and then I want you to give me your opinion."

"You got it," Leon said.

"Disease from the livestock water source, for one thing, although we may want to get Zachariah's thoughts on that. But more importantly, I'm concerned about having some of us wandering around and running into thirdlings in the dark. It may startle the thirdlings and trigger a conflict. So I was thinking we'd wait until morning, and then Desmond, and maybe myself or Zachariah, can walk to the village. Since the thirdlings are already familiar with us, they shouldn't be too alarmed. Desmond can explain—maybe using drawings, something he's already been doing —that we've brought others with us. So by the time the thirdlings see the growing colony here, they'll at least have had a heads-up." She stopped and waited.

"Sounds reasonable to me," Leon said. "What if these thirdlings aren't exactly thrilled to see so many of us squatting on their land?"

Infinity nodded her head. "Then we have to convince them we can be useful."

Leon let out a low whistle. "And you said these things are only half our size? And their village is only 150 individuals?"

"More like a third of our mass," Desmond said.

Leon shook his head. "There's no way they can provide for us. It would be like feeding over 2,000 more thirdlings."

"Now you're starting to get it," Infinity said.

AUGUST 27 - 6:43 AM - Group 12

DESMOND GAVE up trying to sleep and sat up to watch the sun rising over the tree tops. At least with a new refugee group showing up every hour on the hour, he had a rough idea of what time it was. He and Infinity had tried to sleep, but another group would bridge in within minutes, resulting in a repeat of the same noisy confusion and another identical orientation session from Zachariah. And now the sun was up. It was time to go meet with the thirdlings—and then hope for the best.

He glanced over at Lorissa. She was now alone, curled up on her side and cradling her jaw with both hands. Desmond couldn't tell if she was awake or asleep.

"There! Look at that. What are those?" It was a man's voice. The guy stood up.

Desmond turned to look where he was pointing, toward the thirdling village. Camels were walking two-by-two along the road between fenced pastures, at least fifty pairs of them. And a thirdling was mounted on every camel. Desmond's gut tightened.

He shook Infinity's shoulder. "I hate to wake you, but the thirdlings are coming to *us*."

She sat up, immediately alert.

"One of them must have spotted us and gone back to alert the entire village," he said.

The refugees all began standing up, which in itself could have been perceived by the thirdlings as threatening. In fact, the riders at the front of the column saw the wave of humans rising from the grass and stopped to stare. But seconds later, they urged their camels forward. They stopped when they reached the gate to the pasture and dismounted to open it.

Infinity and Desmond got to their feet. She raised her hands above her head. "Everyone look at me and listen! These are the thirdlings we've told you about. I'm not going to lie. The next few minutes may determine whether this colony lives or dies. You *need* their help. Don't be aggressive in any way. I need to know you all understand. Raise your hand if you do."

Over two hundred hands went up. Lorissa was now sitting up,

and she appeared to be the only one with both hands down. But Desmond was pretty sure she was incapable of interfering.

The thirdlings filed through the gate two at a time, coming straight for the mass of humans.

Infinity moved closer to Lorissa and gestured toward the ground beside her. "Gather together and sit here in a tight group."

Mostly silent, they all complied, filling up an area thirty yards across.

The lead thirdlings stopped, and those behind them fanned out and took position shoulder to shoulder. When they were all in place, the entire line moved forward as a unit. Desmond wasn't surprised to see that most of them carried bows with arrows already nocked. He tried to imagine what would happen if the thirdlings attacked. They were outnumbered by humans two to one. But the humans were naked and defenseless. The first few seconds would be a slaughter, although by sheer numbers, some of the humans might charge the thirdlings and pull them from their camels.

"We're counting on their peaceful intentions," Infinity announced, as if she had read Desmond's thoughts. "But if they do attack, we can overcome them. We outnumber them by a factor of two, and each of you is three times their weight. As long as they remain peaceful, don't do anything aggressive. But if they attack, embrace the fear you're feeling and fight for your life. Kill them any way you can. I need to know you understand me!"

A sea of hands went up again.

"I've never been in a fight in my life," a man near Desmond muttered.

The line of mounted thirdlings folded around the humans in a half circle and stopped at about forty yards out. Their singsong voices rippled around the formation as they talked.

Desmond scanned through them until he spotted Jane. He raised his hands and approached her. "Jane, these are my friends. Please don't be afraid, okay?"

When he was fifteen yards from her, several thirdlings to either side raised their bows, ready to pull them back. He stopped, hands still raised, trying to keep his eyes focused on the thirdling he knew best.

"*Bera-noo-noo-noo*," Jane said. She was watching him intently.

"*Bera-noo-noo-noo*," Desmond repeated back. "I'm sorry we disappeared on you yesterday. And I'm sorry I lost the pants you gave me." He smiled and then slowly gestured toward his bare groin.

Her eyes drifted down the length of his body and back to his face. She was not smiling.

A distant howl drew Desmond's attention away from Jane. He turned as two more howls followed the first. The refugees were turning, too, looking toward the perimeter fence. And then Desmond saw them. Three orcs were at the fence, staring through the slats, grunting and howling, apparently infuriated by the presence of humans.

He turned back to Jane and the thirdlings. "Phenomenally unfortunate timing," he said. "I imagine you're learning to associate us with trouble."

At that moment, another commotion arose from the humans. Desmond turned to see twenty fresh refugees floundering for balance and shouting in confusion.

"*Salanoo-too-we-noo!*" cried one of the thirdlings. This was followed by similar shouts from dozens of others. Their camels had also been startled by the sudden appearance of twenty more humans, and many of them grunted and darted out of formation, jostling each other and even knocking some of the riders to the ground.

More howls erupted from the orcs at the fence, and Desmond realized the first three had been joined by more—a lot more.

13

NILOKA-REE-ROH-ROH

August 27 - 7:04 AM

INFINITY TRIED ASSESSING possible courses of action but came up with a fat zero. She was a bridger, not a crowd-control expert. The humans—all 240 of them—were caught between enraged orcs and armed thirdlings. Twenty of the refugees had no idea what was happening, and the rest were on the verge of panic.

If previous experience held true, the orcs would start coming over or through the fence at any moment. The only chance for the refugees was to convince the thirdlings that humans were valuable allies. And Infinity could think of only one way to do that.

"Listen to me!" she shouted. "I know you're scared, and I know you have no weapons. But if you want to live, we have to stop those orcs from getting over the fence. Some of them are probably going to try. If we kill the few that do, that should deter the rest of them. I'm asking you to fight. Every last one of you. Fight to save your colony, to save the human species. Fight for your goddamn life!"

Zachariah was beside Infinity. He spoke softly. "Are you sure that's not suicide?"

She ignored him and glanced at the thirdlings. They were talking rapidly to each other, still trying to get their camels under control. She then turned to the fence, where there were now at least twenty orcs. Three of them were climbing, already negotiating the downturned spikes.

Desmond had backed away from the thirdlings and was now at her side. "Only you would come up with the idea of fighting monsters with our bare hands. I'm scared shitless, but I'm with you."

"And I'm with you, too," Zachariah said.

"So am I," Leon said as he emerged from the crowd of terrified refugees.

Infinity nodded. She then spoke loud enough for the others to hear. "Then that's a start. If the rest of you decide to leave it to only a few, then you're all going to die." She pushed her way through the throng of refugees and ran for the perimeter fence, not bothering to look back. The others would either help or they wouldn't.

The orcs went completely berserk as she approached the fence. They jumped up and down and struck the wood with their fists while howling with rage. Infinity went straight for the spot where three of them were coming over the top, already bloodied from pushing through the spikes. She took a quick glance over her shoulder. Most of the refugees had followed her, and behind them were the mounted thirdlings, looking very much like they were herding the humans to the fence.

She stopped and waited for the climbing orcs, ignoring the almost deafening howls of the others below them. The first orc cleared the top of the fence. Instead of climbing down, he launched himself into the air and dropped the entire twelve feet, landing facing Infinity.

Leon darted around her from behind and went straight for the orc, followed by Desmond and Zachariah. Leon tackled the creature head on, driving it back against the fence. It grabbed Leon's head between its massive hands, lifted him off his feet, and sunk its teeth into the man's throat. And then Desmond struck at its face while Zachariah dove for its legs and wrapped his arms around its knees.

Still gripping Leon in its mouth, it struck out at Desmond, hitting his shoulder and sending him rolling to the side.

Infinity sensed the crowd of refugees coming up behind her, so she leapt at the orc and grabbed its left arm. "Go for its arms and legs!"

Refugees threw themselves at the creature. It hit the fence, staggered to the side, and fell, swinging and growling and taking a dozen humans down with it. It released Leon's limp body and screamed, trying desperately to get its teeth into anything else it could reach. The jostling of bodies forced a man's shoulder too close, and the orc bit into the flesh. The man, who Infinity hadn't even met yet, pulled his shoulder free, losing a fist-size chunk of skin and muscle, and began pummeling the creature's face with his good arm.

The orc hissed and spat and fought like a mountain of muscle, but refugees kept piling on, holding down its arms and legs.

Buried beneath fighting bodies and still holding the creature's left arm, Infinity shouted, "Now kill the son of a bitch! Destroy its eyes and throat."

At least three good-sized men began pounding away at its face, grunting like animals with every punch, relentlessly turning it into pulp.

Screams came from somewhere beyond the pile of fighting refugees, and suddenly the weight of a second orc landed on the bodies above Infinity, nearly crushing her cheek into the ground. The second orc yanked two of the bodies off and threw them both against the fence like rag dolls. As the orc reached down to grab another human, it was swarmed from behind by countless refugees. Under the crushing mass of bodies, it fell to the ground beside the first orc, which had now stopped struggling.

Infinity pulled herself from the orc's carcass and the fighting mass. "You can stop!" she shouted. "It's dead." But her words were lost in the screams and chaos.

"Infinity!" It was Desmond's voice.

She swung around in time to see a third orc land on top of two men. Like an enraged gorilla, it swung both its fists down upon the refugees with deadly force, striking them in a blur until they stopped moving. As more refugees came at it, it picked up one of the men by the head and swung the body, knocking several of them to the ground. Desmond, standing to the side, waited for it to take another swing, and then he rushed in and went to the ground like he was sliding to second base. His leading foot hit the orc's ankle, knocking the creature off balance. And then dozens of humans, including Infinity, were on top of it, driving it to its knees and then to its back. Seconds later, the same three men were on top, striking its face with the powerful blows they had delivered to the first orc.

In the midst of this struggle, Infinity heard an even more terrifying sound—the cracking of a wood fence slat.

The orc beneath her was subdued and would soon be dead, so she rolled from the pile and got to her feet just as the orcs at the fence wrenched the cracked slat in two. Immediately, dozens of orc hands gripped the slat beneath it and began pulling. "I need help here," she cried.

A handful of refugees appeared at her side.

She glared at the main mass of humans who had not yet joined the fight. They were hanging back, obviously terrified. "Get your asses over here, all of you!"

The refugees glanced at each other. Then they moved forward. At first only a few, but then the entire crowd.

"We can't let them come through this fence," Infinity said just as the second slat began to crack. "If they all get through, we're as good as dead. But even if they make the hole big enough, it's still going to be a bottleneck. And we have the numbers needed to kill them one at a time. If we kill enough of them, the rest will give up."

The second board broke, and the orcs pulled it loose. Two orcs thrust their heads through the gap, their eyes filled with rabid hatred.

Infinity took one step and kicked one of them, crushing its nose. Instead of pulling back, it snarled and pushed even harder, the lower slat cutting into its neck.

"They're going to kill us," a woman said. "We can't stop them."

"We have to!" Infinity cried. But she knew the woman was right. They had managed to kill three of the orcs, but if all of these orcs came swarming through the fence at once, the refugees would panic and scatter.

"*Loo-roh-roh-roh. Niloka-ree-roh-roh!*"

Infinity looked beyond the refugees. Most of the thirdlings were back in formation, arranged in a semicircle with their camels shoulder to shoulder. They held their bows ready.

Jane, sitting on her camel in the midst of the formation, sang, "*Niloka-ree-roh-roh!*"

The thirdlings leaned forward, and their camels walked toward the fence, closing in on the humans. Everything became quiet, including the orcs on the other side of the fence as they peered through the gaps, perhaps wondering what would happen next. Infinity looked over at the refugees who had been fighting. They were getting to their feet, standing over three dead orcs. On the ground were seven dead humans, including Leon, and six more that were alive but too hurt to get up.

The thirdlings inched forward, pushing the humans as close to the fence as they could get without the orcs reaching through and grabbing them.

Infinity found Desmond among the others and their eyes met.

He nodded at her as if they had just had some kind of telepathic exchange.

He stepped toward the thirdlings. "Jane, we hope you can see that we're on your side. We can help you."

Infinity studied Jane's tiny face. Her eyes were wide. But they were always wide, so this didn't really mean she was afraid. It was impossible to tell her age, but she seemed slightly more weathered than most of the other thirdlings. From the way the others kept glancing at her, she was obviously important. It was possible that her opinion at this moment could determine the fate of the entire human colony.

"*Loo-roh-roh-roh, niloka-ree-roh-roh,*" she sang, this time much more quietly. She then motioned for the humans to move to the side.

Infinity didn't waste time wondering what this meant. She turned to the others. "Go. Slowly. Don't do anything to alarm them." She pointed to the injured. "Help them up and bring them with us."

The refugees gathered the fallen and shuffled to the side.

Quietly at first, the orcs began snorting, almost like a chant. "*Chuh. Chuh. Chuh! Chuh!*"

The thirdlings advanced toward the fence and pulled back their bows.

"*Chuh! Chuh! Chuh!*" The orcs began pounding the fence, working themselves into another frenzy.

Without any obvious command or warning, the thirdlings released their arrows. Nearly a hundred shafts flew into the fence. About half of them were stopped by the slats, but the rest passed through.

Dozens of orcs screamed in anger and pain, and Infinity could see several of them floundering on the ground. Those that weren't critically injured flew into a rage unlike anything Infinity had ever seen. Instead of fleeing from the onslaught of arrows, they threw themselves at the fence, some of them climbing and others tearing at the partial hole with renewed determination.

The thirdlings nocked new arrows. But now their camels were shuffling back and forth, obviously terrified by the orcs' fury. Another board cracked, and then another crack came from ahead of the shuffling humans. The orcs were working on a second hole.

Another volley of arrows flew into the fence, many of them harmlessly striking the wood. Now the camels were nearly in a panic, and the thirdlings had to fight to get them under control. Another board broke and was pulled away from the first hole. An orc fought its way through the opening, immediately falling and writhing on the ground with dozens of arrows in its body. Another orc came through behind it. This one made it to the nearest camel, pulled the thirdling from its back, and threw the thirdling against the ground before collapsing with arrows in its neck and shoulders. Another orc came through behind that one, and then another. The thirdlings couldn't nock their arrows fast enough.

"Move away from the fence," Infinity ordered. "Toward the thirdling village." She had no idea if the thirdlings would allow them near the village, but there was simply no other choice. The orcs could certainly outrun the refugees, but some might escape by sheer numbers.

The thirdlings pulled away from the fence, with orcs running after them.

"Stay with the thirdlings!" Infinity cried.

The refugees broke into a run, angling toward the retreating camels and riders. But this put them into the line of sight of the running orcs, and the orcs turned and headed straight for them.

As the thirdlings converged on the pasture's gate, the herd of riderless camels blocked their way, obviously terrified and seeking an exit from the pasture. The thirdlings had no choice but to turn and face the pursuing humans and orcs. They quickly gathered into a mass with their bows pointed outward.

Infinity heard a scream and paused to look back. The injured refugees had been abandoned by their helpers, and the leading orcs were just catching up to them. Infinity cried out in anger as the orcs leapt upon the helpless people. It took them only seconds to thrash the injured refugees until they fell silent. The orcs stood over their victims, staring at the retreating mass of refugees as if uncertain what to do. And then they resumed the chase.

As the humans converged on the thirdlings and their camels, the thirdlings raised their bows.

Infinity was ready to order the refugees to stop, but she didn't have to. The entire group came to halt for fear of being shot. They were trapped. She turned around to face the charging orcs. At least fifteen orcs were less than a hundred yards out, running straight for them. And in the distance, more orcs were coming through the fence.

"Please help us!" a woman cried out, pleading to the thirdlings.

The orcs were only seconds away. But they stopped abruptly. They had heard something. They turned and looked back.

"Oh my God," someone said.

And then Infinity saw it. Twenty new refugees—the thirteenth group—had appeared and were floundering at the bridge-in location, crying out in their confusion.

The orcs turned back, apparently deciding the new arrivals would involve less risk than facing armed thirdlings.

Infinity balled her fists and stared. The orcs surrounded the confused refugees. And then they moved in. Screams of pain and terror ripped into Infinity's senses, choking her up and flooding her consciousness with guilt. There was nothing she could do to save them.

As she watched, a figure lifted its head from the grass a short distance from the massacre. One of the orcs spotted the figure and ran over to it. After looking down at it for several long seconds, it slowly kneeled and took the figure's head in its hands. And then Lorissa's cry rose above all the others. Until it suddenly stopped.

"We have to go, Infinity." Desmond was pulling her by the arm.

She blinked and looked around. The thirdlings had opened the gate, and most of them were already through it. Scattered among the camels, the refugees were going with them. And the thirdlings seemed to be allowing it.

14

SHELTER

August 27 - 8:12 AM

THE SLAUGHTERED REFUGEES' screams reverberated through Desmond's consciousness. The fact that the refugees had no idea of the horror they were bridging into made their fate seem all the worse.

For whatever reason, the thirdlings were allowing the two hundred or so surviving humans to take shelter within their formation, interspersed among the walking camels as they approached the village perimeter. Desmond turned to look back at the bridge-in site. A few orcs were still hunched over the slaughtered refugees, possibly feeding on them. But the majority of the creatures—about twenty—were now following the procession of thirdlings, camels, and naked humans. They were keeping their distance, no doubt aware of the lethality of the thirdlings' bows. But occasional eruptions of aggressive screaming made it clear they were intent on continuing their rampage.

He turned to Infinity and Zachariah walking at his side.

Infinity wore a tormented frown. She was no doubt agonizing over leaving the bridge-in site.

"There's nothing we could have done," he said. "The orcs will eventually leave the area. Then we can return to protect the rest of the incoming groups." He tried to sound positive but suspected his despair seeped through.

She shot a glance at him. "There are only two scenarios for that: either we convince the thirdlings to help us defend the site, or we convince them to give us a few hundred weapons. Neither of those are likely."

"But both scenarios are possible," Zachariah said with characteristic optimism. "Particularly the latter of the two. They seem to have an overabundance of weapons on hand. For good reason, no doubt."

As they entered the village, young thirdlings swarmed out the door of the combat-training facility to greet them. But then the kids saw the mass of humans, and they stopped and stared. Several thirdlings sang out a sharp message, and the children ran back inside the structure. The adult thirdlings ordered their camels to kneel, and they dismounted. They formed a line facing the stalking orcs, with their bows ready. They hadn't taken the time to tie off their camels, and the creatures nervously bunched up and began moving parallel to the nearest pasture fence, headed away from the orcs.

The absence of the camels seemed to embolden the orcs somewhat, and they came to within fifty yards of the thirdlings, presumably just out of bow range.

Trying to avoid drawing too much attention from the thirdlings, Desmond and Infinity quietly beckoned the refugees to come together in a tight group behind the defensive line. Desmond worried that at any moment the thirdlings would decide the humans were not their responsibility, and that would almost certainly end in disaster.

The young thirdlings came pouring back out of the training center carrying maces and axes. They came straight for the humans, and for a moment Desmond thought they intended to attack. But instead they stopped in front of Infinity. The nearest one, a boy less than thirty inches tall, smiled at her and handed her a mace. He then turned and handed a copper-bladed axe to Desmond. The remaining kids handed over their weapons, smiling at the refugees as they did so. Then they ran back into the structure. Seconds later, they were back with more weapons, and they handed those out as well.

Now at least fifty humans were armed with maces or axes, perhaps enough to fight off several orcs. But not enough if the orcs came at them all at once.

"This feels damn good in my hand," Infinity said, giving her mace a few practice swings. "We're going back to the bridge-in site. Now."

Desmond frowned at her. "Um, we'd be facing all those orcs at once. More than twenty. Even with these," he held up his axe, "we'd lose a lot of people."

She sighed and turned to look out over the heads of the thirdlings. "Oh, shit."

Desmond looked. The band of orcs was still out about fifty yards. But then movement drew his attention to the distant bridge-in site. Now, in addition to the few orcs that had remained there with the human corpses, another mass of orcs had appeared. It was hard to discern how many, but it looked like the total number of orcs within the perimeter fence had at least doubled. As Desmond stared, the new orcs turned and began walking toward the village.

A flurry of voices passed through the line of thirdlings. Apparently they had realized there were now too many orcs to hold off, and they all began backing toward the center of the village as a group, forcing the humans to retreat ahead of them. The original group of orcs advanced, still keeping their distance but becoming increasingly agitated. The new group of orcs began running, apparently sensing some urgency. They came upon the short camel-pasture fence and quickly scrambled over it. They ran down the road, now only a few hundred yards away.

The thirdlings responded by picking up the pace, headed straight for the stronghold at the center of the village.

"It appears we have a serious problem," Zachariah said. "The thirdlings intend to take shelter in their fortress. Where does that leave us?"

The first orcs were now at the edge of the village, and in seconds the new group of orcs would join them.

"It leaves us alone and exposed," Infinity replied. "We're not waiting until that happens. Listen, everyone! Get into groups of twenty or thirty. Make sure each group has some of the weapons. And then run to the nearest structure and lock yourselves in. One group per structure. Do it now!"

For a moment, the refugees simply looked around like they weren't sure what she meant. Desmond realized the thirdlings might not like this. He found Jane in the line of retreating thirdlings and stepped up behind her. "Jane, I'm sorry, but can we hide in your houses?" He pointed to one of the houses as they walked past it.

She turned to stare at him.

He walked over to the nearest door and reached for its handle. Unlocked, the door swung open to the inside. "There are too many of us," he said. "We'd like to—"

"I said, do it now!" Infinity shouted, apparently unaware of Desmond's attempt at preemptive diplomacy.

The refugees scattered in loose groups, spreading out to the structures. Jane then saw what they were doing. She glanced at Desmond without expression, but neither she nor any of the other thirdlings made any move to stop this invasion of their homes.

Some of the orcs howled. They must have seen the humans

splitting up, because now they were charging through the village. They angled toward one of the refugee groups, trying to head off the humans before they made it to a dwelling. The orcs disappeared behind several dwellings.

"Go, go, go," Infinity cried. "They're coming!"

The thirdlings reached the stronghold and began filing through the door. Jane turned one more time to look at Desmond, but again her face showed no recognizable expression. She slipped through the door and was gone.

A chorus of human screams and orc howls indicated the orcs had intercepted one of the refugee groups. Infinity ran around the edge of the nearest dwelling toward the cries, and Desmond followed. But then they both stopped. The mass of orcs were just catching up to the last of a group of humans desperately trying to push through the door to one of the domed houses. Six refugees were still outside the structure when the orcs fell upon them in a horrifying blur of flying fists and snarling jaws. The humans inside the house managed to get the door shut, but there was no saving those left outside.

"Goddammit!" Infinity muttered.

Desmond looked around. About ten refugees, including Zachariah, were still standing beside the thirdlings' stronghold, apparently waiting for further direction from the bridgers. The others had dispersed to the dwellings and with any luck were safely barricaded. Infinity was still staring at the murdering orcs, even though the human screams had already stopped.

Desmond grabbed her arm. "You can't help them. Come on, let's focus on what we *can* do."

At that moment, one of the orcs spotted them. The creature immediately howled and charged.

Desmond and Infinity ran back to the remaining refugees. "This way," Infinity cried.

They skirted around two dwellings already occupied by

refugees and headed for a larger dome that was likely to be empty. Desmond glanced over his shoulder in time to see four orcs barreling around a dwelling, no more than ten seconds behind them. The larger dome's door wasn't visible, so they ran around the right perimeter and found the door on the opposite side. Zachariah shouldered his way past the refugees who had arrived before him and tried the door. It swung open to the interior. For a moment he hesitated, as if he wasn't sure he should be first, but then he dove through.

"Inside, now!" Infinity ordered.

The refugees crouched and pushed through the opening two at a time.

Desmond heard the orcs coming around the side of the dwelling—heavy footsteps and wheezing grunts. And then they were there, only ten yards away. At first they headed away from the dwelling, apparently thinking the humans had run beyond it. But they stopped and turned.

"Shit," Infinity said. "Go!" She kicked the last two refugees through the door and then dove through. "Get in here, bridger!"

The orcs charged. Desmond's mind locked up. He was seconds from death, and all he could do was stare at the creatures. He stumbled back, pressing against the door frame. There was pressure on his ankle, and suddenly his feet were pulled from beneath him. He fell on his face and was dragged in through the door.

But it was too late. The first orc hit the door as Zachariah was trying to push it shut. Zachariah desperately shoved his substantial weight against the door, but the orc managed to slip its arm around the edge and clamp its fingers onto Zachariah's neck.

Zachariah's feet flailed as he tried to get leverage against the door. "Help me!"

Frustrated howls came from the other side of the door, which was so small that only one orc at a time could position itself to push on it.

Desmond, Infinity, and every one of the refugees converged on the door, piling on top of Zachariah in an attempt to block the orc from pushing it open. Under the pressure of human bodies, Desmond's cheek was pressed against the orc's grimy forearm, and he caught a whiff of feral sweat. He managed to turn his head and then sank his teeth into the creature's arm, biting and pulling until hot blood ran down his chin and into his throat.

"Get his hand off my neck!" Zachariah cried, his voice muffled beneath the pile of struggling bodies.

Desmond shifted his head to the creature's wrist and bit down again, tearing side to side, trying to open an artery, to gnaw it to the bone if necessary. The orc howled with rage and pulled its arm back, finally releasing Zachariah.

The door slammed shut, and someone grappled with the heavy latch until it fell into place.

One at a time, the humans pulled themselves from the pile as the furious orcs pounded and kicked harmlessly against the locked door.

Desmond pushed himself up from the floor and stood looking around the interior of the dwelling. Infinity got to her feet beside him.

"Holy crap," Desmond said.

The floor was littered with wood shavings. In the center of the open space were several short, thirdling-sized tables, each of them covered with freshly-made wooden handles, copper axe blades, and four-bladed mace heads. And against the rounded outer wall were racks of completed axes and maces.

They were in a weapons-assembly shop.

15

PLAN

August 27 - 8:56 AM - Group 14

WHILE THE OTHERS wandered around inspecting the room, Infinity stood at one of the window slits, listening and watching for orcs. The creatures had abandoned their packs and were now roaming freely through the village individually and in pairs. She watched two of them pounding on doors until they found an open dwelling. One at a time, they forced their massive bodies through the tiny doorway. Evidently finding it empty, they came back out a minute or so later and moved on.

Just as she was turning away from the window, the sound of frantic screaming came from somewhere outside.

"Do you hear that?" one of the women asked. "They're getting into the houses."

Infinity moved her ear closer to the window. The screams were too far away to be from one of the village dwellings. Her eyes met Desmond's.

"It's the bridge-in site," he said. "Group fourteen must have arrived."

"But the orcs are here in the village," the woman said.

Desmond turned to her. "Apparently not all of them."

Infinity pressed a hand to one ear, trying to ignore the talking, and pressed her other ear to the window slit. She closed her eyes and listened to the distant screams. She wanted to hear every one of them, to feel the refugees' pain and fear. She at least owed them that. She was the lead bridger for this whole screwed-up effort, and the refugees she was here to protect were being slaughtered.

Warm fingers grabbed her wrist and gently pulled her hand from her ear. "Infinity, stop." It was Desmond.

She yanked her hand from his grip. But then she realized her scalp burned. She looked at her fingertips. The dead portions of her fingernails had been removed while bridging, but the remaining nail stubs had scraped skin from her scalp.

"Are you okay?" He was gazing at her, lines of concern etched on his face.

"We just lost another twenty refugees," she said. "Are *you* okay with that?"

"No, of course not. So let's figure out how we're going to take back the bridge-in site. Otherwise the next group will be wiped out, too. And the group after that." He waved his hand in an arc. "We've got all these weapons."

A huge face darkened the window slit next to Infinity. The orc sniffed the air and tilted its head so it could see in with both eyes. It then spotted Infinity's face only inches from the slit. It grunted and thrust its hand into the window. But the slit was only three inches wide, stopping the orc's arm at the wrist.

Flushed with rage, Infinity grabbed an axe from the rack beside her and swung it at the orc's meaty hand. The blade cut into the wrist, nearly severing it. The orc screamed and pulled back. But the dangling hand jammed in the tight space. Infinity hacked at it again, chopping off one of the fingers, and then the hand was gone. The furious orc pounded at the window with its good hand, but the thirdlings' dwellings were designed for this.

Infinity snatched the severed finger from the floor and threw it through the window slit at the orc. "Ugly son of a bitch!"

Breathing hard, she turned away from the window, screamed, and threw the axe at the far wall. It hit a rack of maces and several of them clattered to the floor. The refugees stared at her as if they thought she might turn her anger on them.

"Infinity?"

She shot a glance at Desmond. She blinked. Then she wiped her eyes. Goddammit. Tears. She couldn't remember the last time she had shed tears.

"We'll make a plan, and then we'll take back the bridge-in site," Desmond said, his voice measured and calm.

She nodded. But it seemed impossible. There were only twelve of them together in this room. The village was crawling with orcs. And how many more had come in through the perimeter fence?

"Let's put our heads together and think about this," Desmond said. "The thirdlings have given us some weapons already. And we have a lot more in here."

"I'll get an inventory of what we have," Zachariah said, and he went to to the nearest rack to start counting.

Infinity took a deep breath and let it out. "We're still probably close to two hundred strong. If we can get a weapon into the hands of every human, and then get everyone together into one group, we could be a formidable force." But the orcs were each at least three hundred pounds of pure muscle. In her head, she envisioned two hundred armed but inexperienced humans walking across the pasture to the bridge-in site. And then she pictured forty enraged orcs charging into their midst, killing humans with their bare fists and ripping their limbs from their bodies.

She paced back and forth, kicking wood shavings with her bare feet. "The last I could tell, there were about forty orcs within the outer perimeter fence. That's too damn many. One way or another, we have to reduce that number. There's a chance we could handle twenty, but not forty."

Zachariah paused in his counting. "What are the chances we could isolate them. Kill them a few at a time?"

"That might be possible," Desmond said. "What if we watch through the windows for a single orc to approach. Then we open the door and call out to it. I'm pretty sure it will come straight for us. After it comes through the door, one of us is ready to shut the door behind it and lock it. And then we kill it. There are twelve of us, and we have weapons. We kill it, and then we do it all over again."

Infinity gazed at the others. Besides Zachariah, there were nine other refugees, six women and three men. None of them looked enthusiastic about this plan. It was likely at least one person would be killed or seriously injured each time an orc came through the door. At least. If they were lucky, they might kill four or five orcs this way, but then their own losses would shift the odds. And if two orcs managed to get through the door at once, well, that would be the end of that.

"Bad plan," she said. "Think it through."

Desmond frowned. But then he shrugged.

Something jiggled the copper door, and they all turned to look. It jiggled again, and then the creature on the other side struck it hard, drawing cries of alarm from several of the refugees. A dark shape passed by the first window slit on the left as the orc moved on.

"I count 71 axes and 89 maces," Zachariah said. "A total of 160 weapons."

Desmond said, "Counting what the thirdling children gave us, that's over two hundred. Enough to arm every refugee."

"One of us can sneak out," Zachariah said. "Go quietly to each of the other dwellings and give them more weapons, then convince each group to carry out the same plan we just discussed. If each group killed only one orc, perhaps that would adequately reduce the numbers."

Infinity faced the nine refugees. "Would you carry out this plan if there were no bridgers there to force you to do it?"

"Not a chance," one of the men said.

Several of the others shook their heads.

Infinity sighed loudly and went back to pacing.

1:01 PM - Group 18

INFINITY STOOD near one of the windows, listening. Although it was difficult to tell, she was pretty sure it had been at least an hour since the last refugee group had arrived. Like all the others, the group had promptly been slaughtered by orcs, their screams drifting across the village to torment her once again. This time might be different. She hadn't seen an orc pass by outside for at least twenty minutes. They had given up and left the village. And since no screams were coming from the bridge-in site, that meant the orcs had finally left the pasture as well.

A smile began to form on her face as she stared through the window, listening. But then suddenly the screams came again, as distinct and horror-filled as they had been every time before. Another twenty helpless refugees, snuffed out by creatures that were now obviously killing them only for sport. Or for hatred of some other species that only came here in the winter and had nothing to do with humans from Infinity's world.

Infinity grabbed an axe and struck the wall, burying the copper blade in the dried clay. She pulled it out and hit the wall again and again until her arm was tired.

"Okay, that's it," Desmond said, walking up behind her. "We're implementing our plan now."

She turned to him, panting. She realized the slaughter of this last group of refugees was her breaking point. She would rather die than allow the orcs to kill one more group. "Damn right we are."

She and Desmond began gathering armloads of maces.

"May I bring up one factor I've been considering?" Zachariah asked.

They both paused.

"Just a thought, although I'd like your assurance that you won't break my jaw." He looked directly at Infinity.

"We don't have time for this," she said and went back to gathering weapons.

"The goal of this colony is to save the human species, is it not?" Zachariah didn't wait for them to answer. "Considering the problems we have already identified regarding the viability of this world, it is quite possible that the colony will have a better chance of surviving with only the existing two hundred souls."

Infinity stopped what she was doing and stared at him. "If I've counted right, group eighteen just arrived. And they were massacred. So another eighteen groups are yet to come. Three hundred and sixty people. What the hell are you suggesting?"

He held his hands up and shook his head. "Never mind. It was just a concern I've been mulling over. I've been trying to do the math, and I can't figure out where all these people are going to live."

"You and the other colonists can figure that out later," Infinity said.

"Indeed. Yes. Later. I apologize. And you can count on me when we attempt to clear the bridge-in site."

Infinity's eyes met Desmond's. Something about his expression suggested he'd been struggling with the same logic. But right or wrong, it didn't matter. There was no way in hell they were going to stay in this room and let orcs kill the rest of the colony. Even if there was a good chance the refugees would all die in the coming weeks anyway.

Infinity turned to the other nine refugees. "Grab as many weapons as you can carry. We're going now."

The plan had actually been Desmond's idea, but the entire group had considered several variations of it before agreeing. And then for several hours Infinity had drilled the others in a few basic skills that might give them a better chance of injuring an orc.

It was obvious the refugees were terrified, but, to their credit, they responded without hesitating and filled their arms with maces and axes. Infinity took one last walk around the wall of the circular room, looking out every window slit for orcs. She spotted none, so they gathered at the door.

"Remember, they look almost human, but they're stupid. Duck low to the side and cut. Duck low to the side and cut. It'll be hard to remember that at the moment you most need to remember it. So I want you to repeat it in your head. Each time you repeat it, visualize the move. Do that over and over again, starting now. And don't stop until we've taken back the bridge-in site." She looked them each in the eye, one at a time. Most of them nodded, and a few moved their lips as they silently repeated the words.

She put her hand on the latch to the door, but then she turned to them again. "There's nothing wrong with being afraid. It keeps your muscles tense and your mind sharp." Actually, this wasn't exactly true. Fear was distracting, and the best fighters were capable of clearing it from their minds. But there was no point in telling them that.

She threw the latch and ducked through the doorway. The August sun was intense, and the air outside was much warmer than inside the weapons shop. The village was silent, and she saw no movement. But that didn't mean it was safe.

"Come on out," she hissed at the others. Soon they were all standing outside the building, loaded with weapons but looking vulnerable and uneasy. "Duck low to the side and cut. Think it and visualize it. Now stay together." She headed to the nearest dwelling. When they were beside it, she put her face to one of the window slits. "Refugees! It's Infinity Fowler."

There was no response. The interior looked empty. So she went to the door and tried it. It swung open to the inside. She turned and looked around at the other structures. The village included at least forty dwellings, and she had no idea which ones the scattering refugees had taken shelter in. This was going to take more time than she'd hoped.

Logically, they should have split up. But their strength was in numbers, so that wasn't happening. She led the group to the next dwelling and spoke through a window slit.

A face appeared in the slit. "We thought everyone else might have been killed," the woman said. "We heard screaming. Are those monsters gone?"

"What's your name?" Infinity asked, ignoring the woman's question.

"Maisie."

"Listen, Maisie. We have weapons and we have a plan to save the lives of the 360 refugees of your colony who haven't arrived yet. But it will only work if every one of us participates. I need all of you to come out and join us. We'll give each of you a weapon."

Maisie hesitated. "You want us to fight again?"

"I want you to live. And I want your colony to live. I need you all out here now."

A man's voice came from beyond the woman's face. "If they have weapons, let's do it."

Maisie looked past Infinity, first to one side and then to the other. "Are you sure they're gone?"

"We haven't seen any in thirty minutes."

Another pause. "Okay, we're coming."

Seconds later, nineteen refugees ducked through the door and squinted in the sunlight. They were each handed a mace or an axe, and Infinity quietly told them to stay together with the entire group.

They moved to the next dwelling, and soon the group grew by another twenty five.

1:50 PM - Group 19

THE MOB of naked but armed humans had grown to 142 when Infinity's original group ran out of weapons to give them. So they moved as a group back to the weapons shop and took every remaining mace and axe. This used up more precious minutes, but the plan required every refugee to be armed.

As they began to move on, in spite of the nervous mumbling and shuffling of feet, a nightmarish crescendo of cries could be heard from the distant bridge-in site.

Infinity paused to listen. She needed to hear every last scream to avoid becoming apathetic to this horrific event that was occurring every hour.

She had hoped they could gather all the refugees before group nineteen bridged in, but it was taking too long to find them. And they couldn't call out to the remaining humans to locate them without drawing the attention of the orcs in the pasture. Their only chance was to stay together and keep moving quietly from dwelling to dwelling.

Just as Infinity was beginning to worry that another hour would pass before they were all together, they came upon a dwelling where twenty-three refuges were hiding, increasing the group to 213. A total of 240 had bridged in before the orcs had appeared at the perimeter fence. Infinity had witnessed twenty refugees being killed, including Lorissa. This meant seven more were either hiding in another structure or had been killed while trying to get there.

Infinity found herself engaged in the same type of cold-hearted mathematics she had criticized Zachariah for. Should she take precious time to find the last seven refugees? Would this lost time cost the lives of the next group to bridge in? And how much stronger would her pitiful army be with only seven additional people?

She gritted her teeth and cursed silently. Bridgers were supposed to take one tourist to a destination world and do whatever was necessary to bring that tourist back alive. She wasn't trained to weigh the value of hundreds of lives, deciding who should or shouldn't live.

"I'm assuming this is all of us," she said to the group, trying to be as quiet as possible. "I need to see the hands of those who were in the weapons assembly shop with me." Eleven hands went up, including Desmond's and Zachariah's. "You've got no more than ten minutes. Take aside a group of twenty and teach them what I taught you in the weapons shop. Duck low to the side and cut. Okay, do it now."

It was a ridiculous scenario. Infinity had been learning to fight all her life. Now she was giving these refugees ten minutes to learn one basic skill before attacking creatures that could easily rip their heads off. But that was the plan. And after hours of mental anguish, it felt good to be trying something.

The terrified refugees did their best. They listened and watched, and then they tried the move. The move was the same whether they wielded an axe or a mace. Duck low to the side and cut. Duck to the left if they were right-handed, to the right if they were left-handed. When it appeared that all the refugees had tried the move about ten times, Infinity stopped the training session and gathered them into a tight bunch. As she had done with the first group, she told them all to repeat the words in their minds and visualize the move. Over and over until the moment they faced the orcs.

To Infinity's surprise, most of them nodded, white knuckles gripping their weapons. They had to be scared shitless, but they all wanted their colony to survive.

It was time to take back the bridge-in site.

16

———————

SURVIVAL

August 27 - 2:27 PM

Desmond gripped the handle of his axe as he and Infinity led the surviving refugees to the village perimeter. The smooth, oiled wood was wrapped tightly with a strip of leather. The leather grip was sized to fit a thirdling's hand, but its presence was enough to give him a feeling of confidence in swinging the weapon. The blade was nothing more than a five-inch copper wedge firmly glued into a hole in the fat end of the handle, but its mass provided devastating momentum when the axe was swung at full force. He glanced at the mace in Infinity's hand. He had used one of the maces but found the axe's lighter weight to be more comfortable.

Desmond blinked and realized what he was doing, fixating on his weapon in order to avoid thinking of the violence that was about to occur.

Infinity stopped the group behind a dwelling at the perimeter of the village where they couldn't be seen by the orcs in the pasture. She tipped her head to signal Desmond to follow her, and the two crept around the edge of the circular dome. They stopped when the bridge-in site came into view. The site was about a quarter mile out, but the mob of orcs was clearly visible. Most of them were sitting on the ground, as if they were simply waiting for the next refugee group to arrive.

"Try to count them," Infinity said.

Desmond started at the left of the assembly. By the time he reached the right edge, he had counted forty-eight, although their density almost guaranteed he had missed some. "At least fifty," he whispered.

"That's what I got. Shit. You see that rise in the field over there?" She pointed to the right. The rise was less than a hundred yards from the orcs. "That's where we're going. We'll circle to the right, and if we're lucky, we can use that rise to surprise them." She turned to him. "Your opinion?"

He gazed at the low bump in the terrain of the pasture. From this angle it didn't seem tall enough. But he had no other ideas. "We'll make it work."

They pulled back to the humans huddled behind the dwelling and signaled them to follow. Using the other domes to shield their movements from the orcs, they made their way toward the edge of the village closest to the rise in the pasture.

As they silently skirted the back side of the last structure, they came upon a handful of thirdlings. Surprised, the thirdlings turned and raised their bows.

Desmond raised his hands and sang in his best thirdling voice, "*Loo-roh-roh-roh!*"

Jane, Bill, and Hickok were among the dozen or so thirdlings, and Jane came forward. Her eyes darted between Desmond, Infinity, and the more than two hundred armed humans standing behind them.

Desmond tried another phrase he had heard Jane use. "*Niloka-ree-roh-roh.*"

Jane sang out a series of new phrases. As she spoke, she pointed out toward the orcs. She then pointed toward the hundred or so saddled camels that had settled into a tight group at the edge of the village in the direction the humans had been moving.

Desmond held up his axe. "We're going to kill the orcs." He swung the axe twice like he was hitting something and then pointed to the bridge-in site. "We hope you don't mind that we're using your weapons." He pointed to his axe with his free hand.

The others sang a few phrases, but Jane just gazed at him.

"We don't have time for this," Infinity said. "Let's move." She began guiding the refugees away.

"We're going to kill them," Desmond said to the thirdlings, and again he pointed to the orcs and swung his axe. "We hope you appreciate what we're about to do. If any of us survive, please take them in and allow them to live here with you." He then backed away from the thirdlings and caught up with Infinity.

"Maybe they'll help us," he said.

She shot him a glance. "I've given up trying to predict what they'll do. They don't think like us."

Infinity guided them around one more domed dwelling to a spot where the herd of saddled camels stood between the humans and the orcs. She and the other humans emerged and crossed the open road that circled the perimeter of the village. They walked into the midst of the camels, which were bunched up against a pasture fence. A few of the camels snorted in alarm, but most of them simply sniffed the humans and popped their lips, creating a shower of spittle. They seemed reluctant to move, and Desmond had to actually push some out of the way.

Beyond the chest-high livestock fence was a small pasture of perhaps twenty acres. A herd of black mammals about the size of pigs was gathered in a far corner of the pasture. As long as those creatures didn't panic and alert the orcs, and as long as the refugees could stay low, then crossing this pasture shouldn't be a problem.

Infinity addressed the entire group. "Get over the fence fast and onto your hands and knees. Don't cut yourself with your weapon. But if you do, don't cry out."

The wood-slat fence was easy to climb, and within a few minutes they were all hunkering low in the grass of the pasture. Desmond raised his head and saw the mass of orcs. The refugees would have to crawl to avoid detection. He turned and studied the humans. Most were now filthy. Sweat ran down their bodies, creating streaks in the grime. Women or men, large or small, black, brown, or white—they all wore looks of frantic determination. At that moment, Desmond had no doubt that every one of them intended to do whatever it took to save their colony. In spite of the dire situation, he felt a wave of pride for his species.

They began crawling across the field. Without clothing, this soon took a toll on his knees. But by the time they were halfway to the far fence, the terrain allowed them to get to their feet without being spotted. Fortunately, the rise Infinity had pointed out was higher than it had appeared from a distance. By the time they reached the fence, the black livestock animals had taken an interest and were slowly walking toward the group of refugees. Desmond had been right—the creatures were similar to pigs. Actually, they looked more like peccaries with unusually long snouts. They were mostly black, but each had a tan chin, and the tan color extended as a stripe up along the shoulder blade on each side. The refugees were over the fence and crouched in the road between pastures by the time the peccaries strolled over to investigate.

Following Infinity's signals, the humans climbed another fence on the other side of the road, which put them into the much larger camel pasture. Now the only thing between the humans and the orcs was the low rise in the terrain about fifty yards away. The herd of camels was nowhere to be seen. Perhaps they had escaped the pasture earlier when the thirdlings and humans had retreated through the gate.

Infinity pressed a finger to her lips, a reminder to all to stay quiet. She waited a moment for several people to relay the gesture. In a low crouch, she headed for the rise. Without saying a word, the entire group advanced.

Soon, over two hundred humans were sprawled in the grass near the crest of the rise. Desmond lifted his head. Gazing through the tall grass stems, he saw the orcs, no more than seventy-five yards away. He even caught a whiff of their musky sweat. The creatures were still sitting in the grass, scattered about in groups of three or four. Sitting cross-legged with their heads down, they appeared to be sleeping. If so, Infinity's plan for surprising them might actually work.

Infinity nudged Desmond with her elbow. "You ready for this?"

He wasn't the least bit ready, but he knew he and Infinity had to inspire the refugees. This was his job now, and he wasn't about to let his partner down. He nodded. "Ready."

She turned to address the others, who were slightly lower on the slope. She spoke barely loud enough for all of them to hear. "Remember, duck low to the side and cut. Think it, visualize it, then do it. Kill those that are closest first. Overwhelm them with your numbers. Don't split off—" Her eyes were suddenly drawn toward the edge of the village. "What the hell are they doing?"

Desmond followed her gaze. It was the thirdlings. Possibly the entire village. They had mounted their camels and were skirting the edge of the peccary pen. Those in the lead reached the far end of the pen and turned on a road separating the pen from the next pasture. This path was taking them directly to the road that ran beside the camel pen.

"They're coming out here," Desmond said. "Maybe they intend to help us."

Infinity was squinting at the approaching thirdlings. "They've given their camels an upgrade."

Desmond watched the first camels coming around the corner

of the peccary pen. Some kind of harness had been added to each camel's chest, with perhaps twenty long spikes protruding to the front and sides like a pincushion. The lead thirdlings stopped at the corner of the camel pasture, and without dismounting they opened a gate. They filed through the gate, headed directly for the humans. As they came through the gate, Desmond could now see that the spikes were made of wood and were about two feet long.

"They're here to help us," Desmond said. "They have to be."

The spiked camels began lining up shoulder to shoulder. About a third of them—perhaps forty—wore the spiked harnesses. When the harnessed camels were lined up, the remaining camels and their riders gathered behind them. And then the entire formation began slowly advancing.

Desmond raised his head and looked at the orcs. They hadn't moved, apparently still unaware of the humans and the approaching thirdlings. But within seconds, the approaching camels would be visible to the orcs over the top of the rise. Apparently the thirdlings were aware of this, because they abruptly stopped.

"What are they planning to do?" Infinity muttered.

Desmond took another peek at the orcs. "If they're here to help us, it could change everything. Let's wait and see."

A sound came from beyond the rise—unmistakably human cries of confusion and surprise. Desmond's eyes briefly met Infinity's.

"Goddammit, it's group twenty!" she said.

They looked over the rise. Like all the others had, the members of group twenty were floundering and retching. The orcs were on their feet and gathering around the new refugees.

"This is it!" Infinity cried. "Remember, duck to the side and cut. Now!" She jumped to her feet and ran over the top of the rise.

Desmond got up and ran after her. Behind him, over two

hundred humans screamed with fury and fear as they charged over the hill.

The surprised orcs turned away from the refuges they had intended to kill and faced the onslaught. For a few long seconds, they stared as if they had no idea what to do.

And then Infinity closed in on the nearest one. Desmond saw her feint to the right but then dart around the orc to the left. Her mace struck the orc's abdomen, and the toothed blades tore a gash so large that intestines spilled out before the orc could cover it with its hands. Infinity went straight for the next orc without looking back.

Desmond pulled his eyes from her to focus on his own attack. He closed the last few yards to one of the orcs and tried reproducing Infinity's move. He feinted to the right, darted to the left, and swung at the creatures gut, making a solid hit. But the orc grabbed his arm and yanked him off his feet. His axe flew from his hand as he was slammed onto his back. The orc dropped to its knees and went straight for Desmond's throat, its mouth gaping. A refugee's axe then cut the creature's forehead wide open.

The screaming human horde slammed into the orcs like a tsunami, axes and maces swinging wildly. Bodies piled over each other, driving the front line of orcs to the ground under the weight. Desmond was buried beneath the mass. The dead orc's head pressed into his chest from the weight. Blood and something much thicker oozed out and onto his neck.

For what seemed like a long time, he could see nothing but struggling legs, arms, and other body parts, punctuated by slivers of sunlight. Screams and grunts were all he heard. But the weight gradually let up as refugees scrambled off the pile. Finally, he shoved the orc's body to the side and sat up.

Before him was the most horrifying sight he'd ever seen. Two hundred naked refugees were fighting for their lives, tearing into the orcs with primitive weapons like savages. At least ten orcs already lay dead on the ground, but beside and on top of them were mangled human bodies. A large shape appeared from the left, an orc leaping into the air. It came down on top of a mass of refugees who were swinging their weapons at a fallen orc, knocking them all to the ground, and began showering them with devastating blows with its fists.

Desmond looked around and found his axe a few feet away. He grabbed it and got to his feet. He circled behind the orc that was pummeling the refugees, darted in, and swung the axe at the thing's back, aiming for the prominent ridge of bulging vertebrae. With an audible *chunk*, the axe cut through the orc's spine. The creature collapsed, its legs convulsing wildly, and emitted an ear-splitting howl. As Desmond was pulling his axe free, one of the men the orc had attacked got to his knees and began chopping at the creature's neck, cutting into it again and again as if he wanted to sever the head.

Desmond turned around. Beyond the struggling, screaming throng of bodies, the twenty newly arrived refugees stared in horror at the chaos. And near the new refugees, at least half the orcs were still standing there harmlessly, gazing at the battle as if contemplating the risks of joining the fight versus fleeing.

"Desmond, look out!" It was Infinity's voice, but before he could turn to find where she was, an orc hit him from the side. He collapsed under the weight and then immediately felt a burning pain in the side of his neck. The creature grunted and pulled its head back, trying to pull the flesh from Desmond's neck with its teeth. Desmond thrashed at it with his axe, but lying on his back made it impossible to inflict much damage. The orc's teeth sank even deeper, tearing through muscle, searching for an artery or his windpipe.

A shape appeared above him, and Desmond realized it was another orc. The creature stared down at him for a split second and then drew back and swung its fist, striking Desmond's temple. It drew back to throw another punch, but then something swept in from the side and hit its face. The object was a bladed mace. Infinity yanked the mace back, and the serrated blades tore most of the skin from the orc's face. She struck again, splitting open its forehead, and the creature collapsed onto the orc that was on top of Desmond. Apparently thinking it was being attacked from above, the orc released Desmond's neck. But before it could even turn its head, Infinity's mace came down on the back of its neck. The impact drove its head down against Desmond's face. In rapid succession, Infinity struck three more times. Each blow shoved the orc's massive face against Desmond's, foul air and spittle erupting from its mouth.

Infinity kicked the top orc off. She then grabbed the hair of the bottom orc and pulled. "Damn, these things are heavy!"

Desmond assisted by shoving the orc. Still dazed from the blow to his temple, he sat up and put a hand to his neck. He felt mangled flesh.

Infinity leaned in and pulled his hand away to see it. "Minimal bleeding. You'll live." She then turned and rushed to help four refugees who had managed to knock a thrashing orc to the ground.

Desmond looked around and realized every orc that was engaged in the battle was facing multiple humans. And those orcs that had not joined the fight—at least twenty—were now retreating, backing away toward the tall perimeter fence. His attention was drawn to movement from the side. The mounted thirdlings had advanced around the fighting orcs and humans and were now charging full speed at the group of retreating orcs. The camels with spikes harnessed to their chests were in the lead, and suddenly the true purpose of the harnesses became clear.

The camels overtook the orcs, plowing into them and skewering them on the spikes. Several orcs immediately succumbed and went to ground. The camels came to a stop and dropped to their knees, driving their chest spikes into the fallen orcs. The camels then stood up, shaking themselves free from the impaled orc bodies, and took off after the remaining orcs. The camels without spikes advanced from behind, and their thirdlings shot arrows into the fallen orcs that were still moving.

Desmond took a moment to help several refugees deliver the last blows needed to kill an unusually large female orc. And then he ran to the group of new refugees. A few of them had finally run out to join the fight, but most were still too confused or frightened to move.

"We need your help!" He cried. "You'll understand later. Grab a weapon from a fallen human and fight. Kill every one of the larger creatures. If you want to survive, do it now!" He grabbed a man and a woman by their elbows and pulled them to their feet. He thrust his blood-soaked axe into the woman's hand. "Take this and fight for your colony." He faced the others. "Go!"

Without staying to make sure they complied, he ran to the nearest dead human—a woman—and picked up her axe. At this point, only five or six of the orcs were still on their feet, and every one of those was surrounded by humans ruthlessly slashing at it with axes and maces.

Desmond joined one of the groups. He immediately felt a twinge of pity for the human-like creature before him. The orc—another female—was still on its feet but wouldn't be for long. Strips of hacked flesh dangled from its arms and body, and each time it swung around to try to deflect a blow, it showered the humans with blood.

Desmond pulled back and let the others finish that one off. He had to remind himself that these orcs had slaughtered seven groups of defenseless refugees, not to mention all those killed during this battle.

He stepped over to a man who was sitting cross-legged beside a pile of bodies, both human and orc. The man was staring down at a nasty bite on his forearm, his mace hanging loosely from his hand.

Desmond kneeled beside him. "Are you okay, sir?"

The man turned to him, his face smeared with dirt and blood, and then Desmond realized it was Zachariah.

"Is it worth this?" Zachariah asked. "Is it even worth it?"

Desmond put a hand on his friend's shoulder. His skin felt cold to the touch in spite of the afternoon August heat. "I think that's a question we can't afford to ask anymore. It's survival. Everything we do from here on is just survival."

Zachariah shook his head and turned away.

Desmond stood up. There were now only two orcs still on their feet. But as he watched, they both collapsed under a barrage of merciless hacking blows. He spotted Infinity. She was walking among the dead and wounded. She paused for a moment, looking down, and then swung her mace twice at a figure Desmond couldn't quite see among the tangled bodies. He hoped it was an orc, although it certainly could have been a refugee she had decided was beyond help.

Orc howls drew his attention to the perimeter fence. Mounted thirdlings were now lined up along the fence to prevent the orcs that had retreated from escaping through the holes. Several orcs were attempting to climb over, but even at this distance Desmond could see numerous arrows protruding from their backs and legs. As he watched, one of them fell. A spiked camel approached it and dropped to its knees, finishing the orc off.

The last eight of the retreating orcs broke away from the thirdlings and ran. Spiked camels caught up to them and formed a semi-circle behind them. The thirdlings angled their camels to one side, forcing the orcs to turn.

Desmond then realized the thirdlings were herding the eight orcs directly toward him and the other humans.

17

RALLY

August 27 - 3:32 PM

INFINITY SAW THE ORCS COMING. The thirdlings were driving them directly toward the refugees. Why in the hell were they doing that? She was about to shout out to all the survivors when a blood-soaked man next to Desmond got up from the ground and spoke up.

"Refugees, listen to me!"

Infinity realized it was Zachariah.

"We have one last chance to show the thirdlings who's side we're on," Zachariah shouted. "If our colony is to survive, we need their help. Let's show them what we're made of!"

Zachariah bent down and picked up a second mace. He then ran straight for the approaching orcs. Desmond followed him, along with most of the surviving refugees, yelling like animals.

"That's what I like to see," Infinity muttered as she took off after them.

When they reached the first orc, Zachariah ducked low to the left and Desmond ducked to the right. Infinity couldn't see what they were doing through the refugees running in front of her, but she did see the orc grimace in pain and go down. And then humans piled on top of it, their arms flailing as they hacked it to death.

The remaining seven orcs were cornered animals, and they flew into the refugees with a fierceness that surprised even Infinity. She skirted around the pile of humans chopping at the first orc and then paused. The scene was so chaotic that she couldn't launch into a full attack on any one orc without hurting some of the refugees. On the left, Desmond and several women faced a snarling orc. That was as good a place to start as any. She ran up and pushed in beside Desmond.

"I'll go for its feet, then push the bastard back!" She dove forward and managed to strike one of its ankles with her mace and wrap an arm around its other leg. "Now!"

Desmond and the others rushed in swinging. The orc grabbed one of the women's arms, and then it fell back, pulling her down with it. The woman screamed as the orc bit her arm and then pulled her closer to go for her head.

Infinity saw a large shape approaching—one of the spiked camels that had herded the orcs. "Pull her back! Pull her back!" She rolled to her knees to grab the woman's feet, but Desmond already had one of her ankles. He grunted and pulled.

The approaching camel dropped to its knees, driving a half dozen spikes through the orc's head and chest just as Desmond pulled the woman free from the orc's grip. The spikes missed her head by inches.

There was no time to check on the woman. Infinity jumped up and saw an orc actually throw a man's body. The body hit another man and spun toward Infinity. She dropped down just as it flew over. The body bounced off the impaled orc as the camel was getting back to its feet, knocking the camel off balance. The camel staggered to the side, throwing the thirdling to the ground, and then stumbled and collapsed on top of the thirdling with the orc's body still skewered to its chest.

Infinity got to her feet again in time to see an orc pushed back until another camel dropped and pinned it to the ground. And a fourth orc had fallen beneath the chopping blows of an overwhelming mass of refugees.

That left four more orcs fighting for their lives.

Two of them were side-by-side, holding off a row of humans trying to press them back. Abruptly, both orcs dove to the ground and rolled under the waiting spikes before the camels could drop to their knees. The orcs got to their feet between two camels and pulled both the riders from their saddles. They threw the thirdlings at the refugees and then turned and ran. Infinity couldn't see where they went through the row of camels, but she glimpsed mounted thirdlings drawing their bows back and shooting.

The last two orcs screamed, and in a desperate move, one of them leapt into the air and came down on top of the mass of human attackers. Several of the humans went down under its weight. In spite of the blows raining down on it, the creature got to its feet and charged through the bodies, trampling over some and pushing others aside. It was headed straight for Infinity.

"Come on!" she shouted, holding her mace ready. But at the last minute, she simply dropped to her hands and knees. The orc tripped over her and went down. Immediately, humans swarmed over it, swinging their weapons. This time, it didn't get up.

Infinity got to her feet yet again. But now the fight was pretty much over. The last orc was hopelessly outnumbered, and it turned to flee. It tried going under the camels' spikes like its companions had, but it was too slow. One of the camels dropped to its knees, pinning it to the ground. Refugees rushed forward to finish it off.

Seconds later, the battle was over. Refugees lay dead or injured on the ground. Those still on their feet glanced around with wild eyes, like they couldn't believe there were no more orcs.

Infinity put her hands on her knees, panting to catch her breath. A few yards away, Desmond sat on his butt, staring at her.

"You okay?" she asked.

He was panting as well, and he just nodded without speaking.

Infinity spotted Zachariah among the refugees. Her eyes met his. "Glad to see you're in one piece, tourist."

He nodded. "And you as well, bridger."

"*Loo-roh-roh-roh!*"

Infinity looked up. It was the female thirdling, Jane. The thirdling loosened a strap between her legs, and the spiked harness, along with two leather straps encircling the camel's front legs, dropped to the ground. She twisted to the side and her camel stepped backwards, pulling its feet from the two loops, and then kneeled. The thirdling lifted one leg over the camel's neck and dropped to the ground.

She came forward, stepping over and around bodies, until she was face to face with Desmond, who was still sitting on his butt.

She spoke to him, her strange words spilling forth like music. Desmond repeated the words back to her, although his voice sounded little like a thirdling's.

She smiled, and Desmond smiled back. She spoke again and pointed toward her village. Infinity hoped she was inviting the survivors, because without at least some rudimentary first aid, most of the injured would become infected and die.

The relative silence was abruptly shattered by cries of confusion and fear. Startled, the thirdlings' camels skittered to the side, clearing Infinity's view of the bridge-in site. Twenty fresh refugees —group twenty-one—floundered awkwardly, falling over each other and over several orc corpses .

Infinity pushed past the nervous camels and approached the new group. Only one of them remained on his feet, a fit man in his forties, perhaps military, or a fighter. The man gazed around at the human and orc bodies strewn everywhere.

As Infinity approached, he turned to her. "What the bloody hell have we bridged into?"

18

―――――――

RITUALS

August 27 - 8:01 PM - Group 25

DESMOND WAS STARING DIRECTLY at the bridge-in site when group twenty-five arrived. Like the previous groups, the new arrivals resembled a nude mob wrestling match for at least a minute before getting their bearings. Zachariah stood to the side waiting for them, and he immediately launched into his orientation speech. The speech now began with explaining why there were 205 human corpses heaped into a pile a short distance from the bridge-in site. Fortunately, this was the last group for which the corpses would be the first horrifying thing they'd see upon arriving. The sun had set a few minutes ago, and it would be dark when group twenty-six arrived. And by the time the last group bridged in at 7:00 AM, the bodies would be buried. At least that was the plan.

"It might become easy for you to conclude that bridging our colony here was a mistake," Zachariah said after finishing his initial explanations. "But there is no turning back for us. There are no do-overs. You need to know that over two hundred of your fellow colonists gave their lives so that you would have a chance. I know that's no easy pill to swallow, but you need to swallow it nevertheless. If our colony survives, those men and women will become the founding heroes of a new human civilization. As will all of you.

"I'm going to tell you what I know and believe." He pointed to about a dozen thirdlings mounted on camels who were apparently there to monitor the situation and perhaps to watch for more orcs. "These are the hominids we call thirdlings. This is their livestock pasture we are occupying at this moment. That's their village you see in the distance. Take a good look at them. They're not human, but they've shown us human-like compassion. Frankly, and for reasons we'll explain later, our colony will not exist without their help. I believe they are not likely to continue helping us unless we can be useful to them. I know many of you have skills that might eventually be useful to the thirdlings. But right now, we think there is one thing they expect us to do for them, and that is to provide protection from those we believe are their enemy." He pointed to the pile of fifty-five orc corpses the camels had dragged to the perimeter fence. "We call them orcs. And it seems our presence here has magnified their aggression. So defending the thirdlings from the orcs may not only be an opportunity for us to fit in, it may be our moral obligation."

"You want us to become bodyguards for another hominid species?" It was a thin woman who was probably close to the upper age limit of sixty.

"It's a job," Zachariah replied. "Regardless of what job you had back home, here you need to be ready to accept any job offered to you."

A lean man stepped forward to stand beside Zachariah. "And that's where I come in." The guy's name was Zeke. He'd bridged in with group twenty-one, just after the last orcs were killed. The guy had a background in hand-to-hand combat training, and during the last four hours he had convinced Desmond, Infinity, and Zachariah that he was going to be valuable to the colony.

"I wasn't here to help kill the orcs," Zeke said, "but I'm pretty sure there are more where those came from." He tilted his head toward the perimeter fence. "And I've got the expertise to train all of you to be badass orc killers. To be honest, I don't give a damn if the job seems distasteful to you. We don't have the luxury of choosing jobs we want. That might come later, perhaps for our children or our grandchildren. But for now, we do what needs to be done." He gazed around at the group before him. "We're going to be so good at protecting the thirdlings that they'll be inclined to provide medical assistance to our wounded, shelters for us to live in, and anything else we need. Notice I said *need*, not *want*." Again, he took several seconds to gaze from one edge of the group to the other. "One last thing. You do anything disrespectful or threatening to the thirdlings, you'll answer to me. You might find yourself banished to the other side of that perimeter fence, and that's not somewhere you want to be."

Infinity plopped onto the ground next to Desmond. Glistening with sweat, she grabbed one of the copper jugs of water the thirdlings had brought out to the pasture and took a long drink. She turned to him. "Let me see that." She tilted his head with her free hand to get a better look at the bite wound on his neck, although there wasn't much to see, as the thirdlings had smeared some kind of greenish salve all over it.

"Still hurts a little," he said.

She shook her head. "Seems hardly enough to exempt you from digging. I swear to God, there's more rock here than soil."

Desmond snorted a laugh. "Sorry you didn't get injured. You're too skilled for your own good."

The thirdlings had sought out every human who was injured—thirty-one in total, minus three that had died in the last few hours—and had moved them to a location near the bridge-in site. Then they had brought out various medical supplies from their village and treated the wounds, even setting a number of broken bones using wooden splints obviously designed for smaller limbs. The medical supplies were primitive by human standards but were far better than nothing and would almost certainly save lives.

The thirdlings had also brought a load of digging tools similar to pickaxes and had put those without injuries to work digging a trench for the human bodies. Surprisingly, none of the refugees had protested this impersonal and dispassionate means of disposing of their fellow colonists. They were beginning to understand that life would never again resemble what they had known before.

For several minutes, Desmond and Infinity sat side-by-side watching the orange sunset fade to deep red.

Finally, she got up. "Break's over. The sooner we get those bodies out of sight, the sooner these people can start putting this day behind them." As she walked away, she spoke over her shoulder. "Enjoy sitting on your ass, bridger."

AUGUST 28 - 6:45 AM - Group 36

A HAND SHOOK Desmond's shoulder. "Hey, you may want to check this out."

He opened his eyes. The sun was just coming up through the trees on the hill to the east. It was essentially the same hill where he and Infinity had taken Zachariah and Lorissa on their first training hike without clothing. But that version of the hill was on a different world, and now it seemed so long ago.

He sat up. It appeared that everyone else was already up. There were now nearly five hundred refugees, and they were gathered around the bridge-in site. "It's almost seven already?"

"You slept at least a half hour that time," she said. "More than I did."

He rubbed his eyes and then gently probed the bite wound on his neck. It was still tender, but less so than several hours ago. The thirdlings' salve was impressive stuff. He looked again at the gathered refugees. "The last group is going to have quite a greeting party."

Infinity got to her feet and stretched. Then she froze. "Desmond."

Her tone instantly alerted him. He got up.

She pointed. "What's going on over there?"

Desmond looked toward the perimeter fence. The pasture was still somewhat dark, but he could clearly see camels lined up in a half circle facing the spot where the thirdlings had dragged the orc bodies.

Without another word, Infinity took off, skirting around the refugees and running for the fence. Desmond followed, visualizing what might happen if more orcs were intending to attack. The refugees still had two hundred weapons from yesterday, but there were now three hundred without weapons.

He caught up to Infinity as they neared the mounted thirdlings. Without hesitating, she pushed her way between two camels and then stopped. Desmond moved in behind her, looking over her shoulder.

Three orcs were actually on the pasture side of the fence. But they weren't attacking. Instead, they were dragging the dead orcs one at a time through the hole in the fence. At least half of the bodies had already been dragged through, and on the far side of the fence, dozens of orcs were watching and waiting. When the next corpse was dragged through, one of the waiting orcs ducked through the hole and grabbed another, dragging it out by its arms.

The thirdlings sat on camels rigged with spiked harnesses, silently watching the process. To the side of the dwindling pile of orc bodies was a stack of new fence slats, presumably to repair the hole.

One of the orcs coming through the hole looked up and saw Desmond and Infinity. It sniffed the air. A low growl swelled from deep in its throat. The orcs on the far side of the fence heard the growl and pushed their faces against the slats, looking through the gaps. They began growling, too, and several of them slammed their fists against the wood.

"Back up," Infinity said. "We're not welcome here."

They pulled back. The camels moved together, closing the gap. Seconds later, the growling stopped. Presumably, the orcs had gone back to their task.

"The only explanation I can think of," Desmond said as they walked back to the bridge-in site, "is that the orcs perform some kind of ritual with their dead, and perhaps the thirdlings respect that ritual."

"Or the orcs eat their dead," she said.

He glanced at her. "Which I suppose could be considered a ritual. I wouldn't have guessed the orcs were intelligent enough for such rituals, though. As far as I can tell, they don't even use weapons. Although they obviously manage to make rudimentary clothing."

"Maybe the thirdlings give them those shorts. They gave *us* shorts."

Again he glanced at her. "Sometimes I marvel at how your mind works. I wouldn't have even thought of that. That would imply that the relationship between the thirdlings and orcs is far more complex than I even imagined."

"They're not human, and they're from a different timeline. Don't expect to understand."

Confused cries could be heard ahead, a sure indication that group thirty-six had arrived. Seconds later, the five hundred refugees gathered around the bridge-in site erupted into cheers.

"That's the last of them," Infinity said. "One more hour and we're out of here."

He gazed over at the completed grave site, now just a mound of dirt and rocks fifteen yards across. Two hundred and five refugees were buried beneath it. Those people had come here for the opportunity to escape certain death.

"Well, at least we know the bridging device is still working," he said. "The SafeTrek building must still be standing."

* * *

7:43 AM - Bridge-back

GETTING MORE than five hundred frightened people to sit together and listen was proving to be difficult, so Desmond and Infinity settled on talking to a core group of those who were calm enough to pay attention: Zachariah, Zeke, and a handful of hard-core survival experts who had shown impressive initiative during the past thirty-six hours.

"We'll never be able to repay what you've done for us," Zachariah said, "but I'm pretty sure we'll never forget. Perhaps someday buildings and streets will bear your names."

Desmond smiled as he pictured this. What might future human cities look like on this world if these people managed to endure long enough to build them? "There's no way to know what will come tomorrow," he said, "but if you can coexist with the thirdlings, you've got a fighting chance."

Infinity turned to Zeke and the others. "Zachariah has proven to be a natural-born leader. He's smart, and he's likable. I don't have any authority to tell you what to do after we've bridged back, but think about that. There will probably be others who want to lead your colony. But if Zachariah has a good-sized group of the strongest refugees supporting him—like all of you—the rest of the colony will support him, too."

Zachariah shook his head. "I appreciate the vote of confidence, Infinity. But there's a good chance we'll have to split up into relatively small groups in order to live among the thirdlings. Having one leader may not mesh with that arrangement."

"Our goal at this time is to train these people to fight," Zeke said. "When we're done with them, they'll be in high demand." He glanced around at the surrounding pasture and beyond. "Based on the layout and size of this village and its land, and assuming the other villages are similar, I'm guessing a pretty convenient partnership is possible. About a hundred humans per village, living together with the thirdlings and providing the protection they need, as well as technological expertise, medical expertise, and whatnot. We'll be sure each group has a diversity of skills."

Again, Desmond smiled. Apparently Zeke was a visionary as well as a combat trainer.

Zachariah looked over Desmond's shoulder and squinted at something. "Heavens to Betsy, would you look at that."

Desmond turned. Five wagons hitched to camels were coming their way. Walking beside one of the wagons were seven humans, all of them wearing bright green shorts.

"I'll be damned," Infinity muttered. "Those are the refugees I assumed were dead."

They walked out to meet the refugees and the wagons.

"We're glad to see you survived," Zachariah said to them. "We tried finding you but ran out of time. I imagine you'll consider yourselves lucky when we explain what you've missed." He then led them away toward the main mass of people.

The doors on the armored wagons opened, and thirdlings swarmed out carrying steaming copper pots. The smell of cooked meat hit Desmond's nostrils, making him realize how hungry he was. Unfortunately, he was pretty sure he wouldn't have time to eat.

Jane, Bill, and Hickok came forward and stopped before Desmond and the dozen or so humans gathered around him. Jane's eyes drifted through the large colony of refugees. Although thirdlings and humans shared few facial expressions, Desmond was almost certain he could see bewilderment in her eyes. As in, *What the hell are we going to do with all these naked, brutish creatures?*

Desmond stepped forward. "Jane, did you bring your book and your pen?" He made motions of writing on a page. "I'd like to try to explain to you how humans can help you and your friends in the other villages."

She watched his fingers moving and then looked into his eyes. But then she was gone, along with everything else.

19

————————

PASSERINA

August 28 - 8:01 AM

INFINITY LANDED ON HER FEET, quelled her urge to retch, and then paced back and forth, waiting for Desmond to get past the worst of his nausea.

"Welcome back," Armando said over the comm. "I can't begin to express my relief at seeing that you both appear to be well."

"We're okay," she said. "We'll need antibiotics, especially Desmond. He's got a wicked bite on his neck."

Several techs came in through the airlock. Responding to Infinity's words, they went straight to Desmond, asked him a few questions, and led him out.

"What news of the colony?" Armando asked.

She shook her head. "Not good. We lost over two hundred before we got things under control."

"Jesus! What happened?"

"Exactly what I said might happen thirty-six hours ago! But

Eagleton insisted we bridge the colony anyway. Where is that bastard?"

"He's meeting with Viper and Falcon as we speak. You're not going to like what he's telling them, Infinity."

"What?"

"In fifty-six minutes, we're sending out another bio-probe. The bio-probe will return at 9:00 PM tomorrow night. If it comes back positive, we're sending Viper and Falcon at 10:00 PM, along with the first group of refugees."

She stared at him through the plexiglass. "Refugees? What about the assessment excursion?"

"To save time, we're eliminating the assessment excursion. From here on out, after any successful bio-probe, we're sending a colony. All 718 refugees."

For several seconds, Infinity couldn't even come up with anything to say. "That's... goddamn insane!"

He shook his head. "Conditions are getting worse by the day. It's not as insane as you think."

Two techs came back into the chamber and began leading her to the med lab.

"There's something else I need to tell you," Armando said.

She turned and waited.

"Trencher and Wraith are sick—something they picked up on their last excursion. Our med techs still don't have a handle on it. So after Viper and Falcon complete their mission, you and Desmond are up again. And as I'm sure you've surmised, you will not be allowed an assessment excursion."

August 28 - 7:43 PM

· · ·

LENNY STRODE the length of his bunk room and back without his crutches. "Are you impressed? Two more weeks, Des! Maybe only one with good behavior. Two more weeks and Xavier and I can join a colony. Infinity, I don't know where you guys got your med techs, but they are zip-banging awesome!"

"I can't argue with that," she replied. "They've saved my ass a few times." She decided not to tell Lenny and Xavier that she was beginning to doubt the SafeTrek building would survive another two weeks.

Desmond said, "Okay, then I'd like to propose a plan. At some point, when the end is near, Infinity and I will permanently bridge out with the last colony. If you two haven't already bridged out with an earlier colony, you're coming with us."

"Cool," Xavier said.

Lenny raised the white flask he'd been carrying. "That, my brother, is a wicked-crisp idea." He took a drink and passed the flask to Infinity.

She shook her head, so Lenny extended it to Desmond. Desmond took the flask, but then he glanced at her.

Curious to see how he'd respond, she gave him a disapproving frown. He hesitated and then passed the flask to Xavier.

Xavier accepted it, but he was eyeing them both. "Geez, you two. You've progressed to nonverbal communication. What's up with that?" He then took a long drink.

"What that means," Lenny said, "is that Desmond got the girl. You and I never had a chance, Xavier." He snatched the flask from Xavier and then turned to Infinity. "Since it's the end of the world and all, have you two—you know—hooked up yet?" He made a stupid fist-pumping gesture with his hand.

Infinity leveled her gaze at him. "You're stepping over the line, tourist."

He immediately wrinkled his brows and shook his head. "Sorry. I've had a few snorts of this." He raised the flask slightly. "Sometimes my mouth speaks before my brain has even hit the snooze button, as they say."

"No one says that," Xavier muttered.

Infinity gazed at Lenny without cracking a smile, although it wasn't easy. But she couldn't help wondering if '*hooking up*' with Desmond would ever be possible. Probably not before they were all killed.

Lenny said, "When Xavier and I heard you guys made it back alive, we decided to celebrate. God knows, there sure isn't anything else to celebrate these days."

"Unless you wanted to have an end-of-the-world party," Xavier added.

"You two are going stir-crazy," Desmond said. "But enjoy it while you can. If you end up bridging out with me and Infinity... well, our track record isn't too good. You may wish you were back here waiting for the Earth to implode."

Lenny raised the flask. "I'd follow you anywhere, Des. Even if it means going to hell."

AUGUST 31 - 9:52 AM

INFINITY ENTERED the chamber viewing room and stopped between Desmond and Armando.

"Where is he?" she asked.

They both knew she was talking about Reece Eagleton. The son of a bitch had been avoiding her since she and Desmond had bridged back.

"You might as well stop asking," Armando replied. "He has no desire to engage in an argument with you. For that very reason, he's not here. But there are two people here I'd like you to meet." He turned around and gestured to a man and woman Infinity had hardly noticed when she had come in. "Andrea Van Loon and Gavin Pushing," Armando said. "They were originally selected as representatives of their colony for the assessment excursion. But that was before assessment excursions were nixed. Now they're simply, well, representatives of their colony."

The woman, Andrea, extended her hand. "We're pleased that you'll be assisting our colony, Infinity. We've heard so much about you."

Infinity shook her hand, assessing her grip and studying her eyes. "Then you're aware of the questionable success of the colony Desmond and I recently bridged. What's your opinion of that?"

She paused for a moment but didn't seem to lose confidence. "My opinion is that the colony should have selected a destination with a recent divergence point. If the world had been more similar to ours and occupied by humans, they would all probably be alive."

The man extended his hand. "That's why our colony, from the beginning, has desired to bridge to a world that has only recently diverged from our own. One hundred and fifty years, to be precise, due to our desire to avoid encountering ourselves or our parents."

Infinity shook his hand. "Sounds reasonable."

Gavin slapped his somewhat flabby gut and shook it. "As you can probably tell, Andrea and I weren't selected as colony reps based on our fighting or wilderness survival skills." He glanced at the woman. "No offense, Andrea." He turned back to Infinity. "Those skills will not be needed where we're going. I happen to be a defense attorney, but I am best known as a motivational speaker."

"And I am a human rights advocate," Andrea added. "And also an attorney."

Gavin nodded. "Our primary role will be to convince the authorities of our new world that it is their moral responsibility, as well as their civic duty, to provide our colony asylum."

Infinity nodded slowly, still studying their faces. "But I assume your colony includes at least some experts in combat and wilderness survival? You know... just in case."

Andrea flashed a polished but annoying smile. "Our colony began with a core group of like-minded politicians and civic leaders, who then hand-picked the remaining members to meet the necessary requirement of 718 talented people. We have no intention of fighting for survival or living off the land."

Infinity glanced at Desmond. "Because what could possibly go wrong."

"Excuse me?" Andrea said, slight annoyance in her voice.

Armando cleared his throat. "Infinity."

"Never mind," Infinity said to the two attorneys. "Desmond and I will do our best to help you bridge safely to your world."

Celia Pickett's voice came through the comm. "Viper and Falcon will bridge back in one minute." Although Celia was Armando's assistant, she was now pretty much running things about half the time. A necessity, as the bridging device was being activated every hour on the hour and would continue to do so until the end.

Infinity turned away from the motivational speaker and the human rights advocate to peer through the plexiglass window. She tried unsuccessfully to suppress her apprehension. Only thirty-six hours ago, following a successful bio-probe, Viper and Falcon had bridged out with eighteen refugees. They hadn't been allowed an assessment excursion. And then thirty-five more refugee groups had been dumped onto that world. With no real knowledge of what they were bridging into. To a world with a 500,000-year divergence point.

"Ten seconds," Celia announced.

Infinity pressed her hands to the window and whispered, "Please be okay, brothers."

The plexiglass bulged out slightly. Two figures appeared and dropped to the padded floor.

Infinity stared at them. "They're not moving. Get the goddamn med techs in there!"

The airlock opened and four techs in white biosuits rushed in, two of them kneeling beside each bridger. Viper and Falcon appeared to be without serious injuries, but their skin color wasn't right. And as Infinity stared, she realized their bodies displayed rigor mortis.

"Jesus, they're dead," Desmond said.

Infinity slammed her hands against the plexiglass and then paced back and forth in the small viewing room. She had worked with Viper for three years and Falcon for over two. They were good bridgers. They were like family to Infinity. Trencher and Wraith were still sick, quarantined in an airlocked chamber adjacent to the med lab. According to rumors, they were afflicted with horrific lesions and fever, which meant it was likely the 718 refugees they had assisted were suffering the same fate.

So Infinity and Desmond were now the only two experienced bridgers at SafeTrek.

"Both bridgers are deceased," one of the med techs announced through the comm. "Cause of death will have to be determined by autopsy. But we're guessing the time of death to be approximately thirty-six hours."

Infinity swung around to face Armando. "They died as soon as they bridged in! And then you sent an entire colony to that world. If you'd done a damn assessment excursion, you would have known not to send the colony."

Armando raised his hands, palms up. "The bio-probe animals came back alive, Infinity. Logically, Viper and Falcon should have bridged into a safe world. Besides, you know my hands are tied on this. It comes from President Millwright."

She allowed a growl to escape from deep within her. "Yes, but how much have you fought against it?"

He actually looked hurt. "You don't think I've resisted?"

She just shook her head without answering.

"Infinity, on some level you have to see that they're right. We're running out of time."

She turned away from him and pressed her forehead against the window. The techs were already wheeling the bodies of her brothers to the med lab. Silently, the two colony reps left the room. Armando put a hand on Infinity's shoulder for a moment and then stepped out. Desmond moved to her side until their shoulders were touching. The contact felt good.

They stared into the bridging chamber as the minutes passed. Techs entered the chamber and disinfected the floor. Voices spoke over the comms, providing updates on recharging the bridging device's power center and counting down to its next activation. Forty minutes. Thirty-five. Thirty.

Twelve animals were brought into the chamber in pairs: sheep, rabbits, domestic cats, guinea pigs, rats, and mice.

Several techs stayed in the chamber until the last minute, holding the larger animals in place and keeping them calm. At sixty seconds, they let the smaller animals out of their wire cages, carried the cages out of the chamber, and sealed the hatch. The creatures stood in place, sniffing the disinfectant still drying on the floor.

Celia counted down the last ten seconds, and then the animals were gone.

Still, Infinity and Desmond stared into the chamber. He moved slightly, causing the skin of his arm to glide over hers. She turned to gaze at him. They had thirty-six hours before the bio-probe returned. After that, all bets were off. The nightmare would start all over again.

He turned to face her. His eyes drifted down to her chest. He reached out and traced the outline of her painted bunting tattoo with the tip of his finger. "This is getting faded again. Are you going to have it re-inked one more time?"

She shook her head slightly. "No point now."

"Passerina," he said. "Is it okay if I call you that?"

Passerina was the scientific name of the bunting. It also happened to be Infinity's real name.

"Yes," she said, surprising herself. "But if you do it in front of others, you're a dead man."

The corners of his mouth barely turned upward. "I'm glad I'm your partner, Passerina."

She took his hand and led him toward the door. It was time to do a few things she had been putting off for too long.

AUTHOR'S NOTES

This story is based on the idea that non-human hominids proliferated and spread throughout the world, establishing complex societies. This is not as far-fetched as you might think. Let's imagine you could see the results of an evolutionary do-over of the last 210,000 years (which is exactly what Desmond and Infinity see in this story). The species, *Homo sapiens* (that's us), first appeared in Africa about 200,000 years ago. At that time, there were other hominid (human-like) species, including *Homo neanderthalensis* (Neanderthals), *Homo Erectus*, and *Homo heidelbergensis*. And possibly others.

There was no guarantee that *Homo sapiens* would survive. In fact, at one point about 80,000 years ago, *Homo sapiens* almost went extinct. It was during a severe drought (as indicated by fossilized mud cracks in an old African lake bed). The climate in Africa was highly variable at that time, and there were many factors that could have resulted in the demise of *Homo sapiens*. And so it's quite reasonable to imagine that *Homo sapiens* could have gone extinct, or that some random event could have prevented their origin in the first place.

If *Homo sapiens* hadn't survived, it seems very possible that one of the other hominid species could have developed a similar level of intelligence. This is exactly what happened with Neanderthals, although they eventually went extinct. Perhaps it could have even been *Homo floresiensis*, the 3-foot "hobbits" that lived on an island in Indonesia about 190,000 to 50,000 years ago.

Okay, what about the rather mind-bending concept of the possible existence of infinite parallel universes?

While there are certainly cosmologists who are skeptical of the concept, it is important to point out that multiple parallel universes is not a *theory*. Scientists did not simply come up with the idea using their imaginations. Instead, the concept is a mathematical consequence of our current theories in physics, particularly *quantum mechanics* and *string theory*.

If we assume that quantum mechanics and string theory are not completely wrong, then it is important for scientists to examine all of the mathematical consequences of those theories. Even if those consequences (such as parallel universes) seem strange to us. This is often how science moves forward.

There are at least five plausible scientific theories that suggest the existence of multiple universes (the "multiverse"). My favorite of these is the concept of "daughter universes" suggested by the theory of quantum mechanics. Quantum mechanics describes things in terms of probabilities, rather than definite outcomes. The mathematics of quantum mechanics suggest that every possible outcome of every situation actually occurs—in its own separate universe.

Everything is made up of tiny particles, and what this "daughter universes" concept boils down to is that there could be infinite parallel universes, each of them differing by the position of only one particle.

The concept boggles the mind. But it certainly makes for a fun story.

ACKNOWLEDGMENTS

I am not capable of creating a book such as this on my own. I have the following people, among others, to thank for their assistance.

For this book I had editing assistance from Josiah Davis (JD Book Services). Josiah provided numerous suggestions and helped me to polish the finished product.

My wife Trish is always the first to read my work, and therefore she has the burden of seeing my stories in their roughest form. Thankfully, she does not hesitate to point out where things are a mess. Her suggestions are what get the editing process started. She also helps with various promotional efforts. And finally, she not only tolerates my obsession with writing, she actually encourages it.

I also owe thanks to those in my Advance Reviewer group. They were able to point out numerous typos and inconsistencies.

Finally, I am thankful to all the independent freelance designers out there who provide quality work for independent authors such as myself. Jake Caleb Clark (www.jcalebdesign.com) created the awesome cover for *Bridgers 2: The Cost of Survival.* Najla (najlakay on fiverr.com) created the cool map of the bridge-in site.

ABOUT THE AUTHOR

Stan Smith has lived most of his life in the Midwest United States and currently resides in Warrensburg, Missouri. He writes adventure novels and short stories that have a generous sprinkling of science fiction. His novels and stories are about regular people who find themselves caught up in highly unusual situations. They are designed to stimulate your sense of wonder, get your heart pounding, and keep you reading late into the night, with minimal risk of exposure to spelling and punctuation errors. His books are for anyone who loves adventure, discovery, and mind-bending surprises.

Stan's Author Website
http://www.stancsmith.com

Feel free to email Stan at: stan@stancsmith.com
He loves hearing from readers and will answer every email.

That's right—*Bridgers* continues. Infinity and Desmond have so much work to do. Be sure to check out the next book in the series:

Bridgers 3: The Voice of Reason.

A devastated world. A desperate colony.

As Earth's destruction approaches, bridgers Infinity Fowler and Desmond Weaver wrestle with the fact that eight billion people are about to die. While on the road to see Desmond's mother one last time, they witness chaos like nothing they've ever seen.

Infinity and Desmond must fight their way back to SafeTrek to fulfill their primary duty—saving the human species. Their next mission: bridge 718 civic leaders to an alternate world. They'll then have thirty-six hours to help the refugees find their place in this new world, after which the bridgers will return to SafeTrek—assuming the building hasn't collapsed.

But when the bridgers and refugees arrive, they don't find the civilized world they had expected. Instead, they find a ravaged planet where humans are forced to live in caves and fight for scraps. They discover creatures that shouldn't exist and weapons that do worse than kill.

How can a colony so ill-prepared for these conditions possibly survive? In their desperate attempts to prepare the refugees, Infinity and Desmond face challenges that threaten to change them forever.

www.ingramcontent.com/pod-product-compliance
Lightning Source LLC
Chambersburg PA
CBHW060418310726
48976CB00003B/1109